BLACK AROUND THE EYES

a novel

JeremyAkerman

Cover image by the author
Cover design: Rebekah Wetmore
Editor: Andrew Wetmore
ISBN: 978-1-990187-36-0

MacLelland and Stewart first published this book in 1981. Moose House published this revised edition in June 2022.

2475 Perotte Road
Annapolis County, NS
B0S 1A0
moosehousepress.com
info@moosehousepress.com

We live and work in Mi'kma'ki, the ancestral and unceded territory of the Mi'kmaw People. This territory is covered by the "Treaties of Peace and Friendship" which Mi'kmaw and Wolastoqiyik (Maliseet) People first signed with the British Crown in 1725. The treaties did not deal with surrender of lands and resources but in fact recognized Mi'kmaq and Wolastoqiyik (Maliseet) title and established the rules for what was to be an ongoing relationship between nations. We are all Treaty people.

Foreword to the 2022 edition

Over 400,000,000 tonnes of coal have been taken out of the ground on Cape Breton Island from as many as 300 individual mines, 12,000 men being employed at the industry's peak. Around 2,400 of them died in mine accidents of various kinds, the most tragic being an explosion in Number 12 colliery in New Waterford in 1915, when 65 men were lost.

In 1981, when this book was first published, there were only a handful of collieries remaining and the workforce was down to around 3,000. It was also the year in which the last strike occurred in District 26 of the United Mine Workers of America.

However, there were still many men alive then who had lived through troubled times in the industry and more than a few who had witnessed the 1925 strike, the focal point of the book. It was from those men that I heard many of the anecdotes I included in this story. To them I shall be forever grateful.

Apart from a few small, illegal, "bootleg" mines, there are no coal mines operating in Cape Breton today. There is nobody who remembers the 1925 strike. They are all dead.

But what men they were! What lives they led! Their story is as inspiring today as it ever was.

The notion that men working long hours in a dangerous occupation would make time for union and political action is still uplifting. For theirs was a cause worth fighting for. No thinking, feeling person could not have been a Communist in 1925. The wages were so miserable, the working conditions so appalling, the living environment so austere and precarious it is little wonder they dreamed of a better world without want and unfairness.

For those interested in learning more, Cape Breton University archives has a recording of a documentary I made in 1967 for CHER Radio, Sydney, about the 1925 strike. It features the voices of some of the men who were there relating what they saw.

I am as proud of that documentary as I am glad I wrote this book. It allows me to relive the wonderful hours I spent with Al, Archie, Gordon, Frazer, Will, Billy, Dancer, Bucky, Walter, Murdock, Johnny, Eddie, Jookum, Pius, Mickey, Clicky, Peter, Skinny, Bunny, Moose, Shelly, Joe, and Placide. A breed of men whose like has passed from the face of the earth.

JBA, 2022

Also by Jeremy Akerman

What Have You Done for Me Lately? *A politician explains*

> Lancelot Press published the first edition in 1977. Moose House published the revised edition in 2022.

Outsider *a memoir*

> Published by Moose House in 2022.

This is a work of fiction, set in a very real place and time. The author has created the characters, conversations, interactions, and events; and any resemblance of any character to any real person, apart from those acknowledged in the author's note on page 255, is coincidental.

Contents

Jeremy Akerman

1: Like a porcupine

I've got the letter in my pocket now. Damn near illiterate it is. There's no excuse for anyone sensible to write like that, especially not if they had a bit of education. Problem is the younger people don't read like I did; they barely skim through the *Cape Breton Post*, and then only the sports and entertainment pages half the time. Still, I guess if I had been keen on encouraging the kids like Daddy was with me, it might have been different. Only got myself to blame for that maybe.

Illiterate or not it's quite the bombshell! I never thought a piece of paper could cause so much confusion, set the family one against the other and, now I come to think on it and admit it to myself, prick the pride of an old man. Imagine! Ruby thinks I'm so old and foolish that I can't take care of myself and need to be under her eagle eye every minute of the day. Maybe she thinks I go around here falling in the gutter and pissing my pants. Damned if I like that kind of suggestion one bit. I may be eighty, but by Jesus I'd go a round with some of these young punks and I'd easy race our Ruby around the block, her with her big fat arse!

If it hadn't been for the impertinence I might have given in right off the bat and gone along with what the wife wants. But stubborn's one thing I always was. Getting past it, indeed! Over the hill she thinks I am. Well, they can all just sweat it out for a while until I'm good and ready.

"Well, old man," Marg had said to me, putting it in and twisting it a bit, "have you made up your mind yet?"

I stopped staring into my dirty old chipped mug of tea and looked over to where she was standing, hands on hips, by the kitchen table. Really snarky. She reminds me a bit of Ma when she gets on her high horse.

"'I won't be rushed now," I said deliberately, "so don't be trying to rush me."

"By the jumpins!" she exclaimed hotly, "it's three weeks or more since we got the letter and still he can't make up his mind. How long will you need? All year?"

The more they push, the stiffer I get. I'm a contrary old bastard at the best of times, leastways if you listen to the kids on the street, but when those christly women get to their needling and shoving, I'm like a porcupine.

"As long as it takes and no shorter," I spluttered into the strong tea, now cold and bitter, because I knew it annoyed her. "Leave me be, woman, I'll decide by and by."

"It'd only be fair to Ruby and Tom to let them know soon," she persisted, rubbing her shiny red hands on the front of her apron, knocking flour dust and small threads of dough to the floor. "Only fair."

She gave me the what-better-could-l-ever-expect-from-the-likes-of-that eye, waiting for an answer.

"Fair!" I snorted and gave the tea another loud gurgle.

"Listen to that! No wonder you don't want to leave this dump. Happy like a pig, slobbering and snuffling over your food and drink. You're just like everybody else around here."

"Yes, I am," I said, starting to get really riled up now because she was beginning to sound like my mother, who always thought herself a cut above the neighbours, "and so are you, Marg MacPhee, even if your father did wear his necktie to bed!"

"Insults now, is it? If you're going to be a fool, I guess I you may as well be an ignorant fool! For the love of God, man, we've only got a few years left, the pair of us, and you want to spend it here! What's wrong with a bit of comfort, for God's sake, and being with our daughter and grandchildren?"

"Who said there was anything wrong with it?"

"You may just as well say there is, the way you've been acting the last going off here!"

"Damn you, woman." I was wrathful. "Do you suppose it's easy for me? If you think a hut in the concrete jungle is some kind of paradise to spend your last days in, you go and leave me in peace."

"So! You have made up your mind after all. I guess I should be grateful for a decision of some kind." She tossed her head the way Ma did when Daddy and me we were in union trouble, and turned away with a sniff.

"'For the last time," I said, trying to be very quiet about it, although my blood was really boiling, "I've not made up my mind yet. When I do, you'll be the first to know. But I'll tell you this, my girl, living with Ruby and Tom isn't the dreamland you think it is."

"Who'd have thought the great world traveller would be scared of Toronto?" she sneered.

"World traveller, my arse! Now you're really sounding foolish, woman. I bummed around this country a bit and went to England in the war, that's all, but at least I've been some place."

"Yes, and you whored around and got filthy drunk in all of them, I shouldn't wonder!" She snapped like a garter belt.

Bite your tongue, I said to myself, and, ignoring the remark, rose from my old chair, put on my cap and coat and marched out into the wind.

I paused at the gate, creaky and shabby as ever, and looked through the thin mist up then down the row where I have lived nearly all my life.

What things this old row of shacks has seen! It seems to have changed very little. Still children by the score, snotty nosed and noisy as bedlam. A new house or two; a few new coats of paint, but not many. Two houses torn down, one burned down. A bit of asphalt on the road. Dogs still rooting around, yelping and gambolling with the kids, tripping people up, running after cars, slobbering on your boots. Carved out of the barrenness eighty years or more ago, and since then: marches, strikes, one murder, hundreds of fights, wakes by the dozen, showers, drunks and drunkenness with me contributing my own share—lines of laundry, smells of cabbage and turnips, smiles of red-faced women, sunshine, snow, always wind, and Crooked Billy spitting into the gutter.

"Billy!" I called into the gust. "Wait up, b'y!"

"Good day, Donnie," he croaked, swivelling around on his old crutch. "Where'd you be going?"

"Down the shore. Walk with me to the end of the row."

"Sure," he said, chewing his lips like he was getting ready to tackle a Christmas dinner. "I heard you was going to live away. In Tronno."

"Well, you may have heard right," said I, but adding too testily, for Billy was one of the best you could find, "and then again you may have heard wrong."

"Makes no mind to me, b'y."

"Our Ruby wrote and asked for us to go and live with them."

"What does she say about that?" Billy nodded his head in the direction of the house.

"She's all for it, wouldn't you know?" I put up my collar against the chill. "Wants to be close to Ruby, I guess."

"For the love of Jesus, why don't you go?" He spat violently in front of us. I side-stepped to avoid it. "What's keeping you around here?"

"Eighty years," I said morosely. "Home."

"Home! Some home!" He spat again. "Go and take it easy."

"I'll think on it for a while yet."

I left Crooked Billy at the corner and came on down here to this cliff where it's quiet, save the wind and wheeling of the gulls, and a little splashing of the sea where it crinkles along the gravel and bubbles in behind those big green rocks.

I guess I shouldn't be so hard on the old woman, but if she wouldn't rub me the wrong way I wouldn't be so cranky. It is not so hard to understand the way she feels, being away from the grandchildren. They are growing up fast now and the eldest will be fifteen or sixteen soon. I guess Ruby won't see forty-five again and that thing she's married to is fifty if he's a day. Not that she really deserved any better because she was never what you'd call a raving beauty and she certainly wasn't a mental heavyweight. He is what Ma used to call a "good provider," suited and tied all the time, good job, lots of pay, padded pension plan, votes Liberal, head of the Lions or the Tigers or something. Problem is if he cut himself he could bleed to death without anybody knowing, they'd think it was water flowing down his arms.

"Very well mannered," Marg says.

What she means is he is not like me, with my rough and ready Cape Breton ways which, just to get her going, I exaggerate a bit now and then. No devilment in Ruby's Tom, that's for sure!

Gordie MacPherson used to say that Ontario

people didn't have much blood in their veins, anyway, and Ruby's Tom certainly doesn't. Unemployment forces Cape Breton girl to big city. Insurance manager marries secretary. That sums it up in headline form, as they say.

Marg has missed her all this while, there's no doubt about that, and I'm sure she wouldn't mind being fussed over and waited on. Not that it'd last; a few weeks at most and she'd be washing the laundry and baking bread and trying to take over from Ruby. If there's anyone should know what can become of that kind of situation, 'tis my Marg, but there's none so blind as those who won't see.

Will, now he's different. This place is in his soul and he's an independent sonofabitch into the bargain. He's active in his local union, has stayed single just as long as I did, and has the courage of a bear. He came along a good while after Ruby but he wasn't spoiled and he worked hard. He's one of those fellows -and they are a good many of them, contrary to popular opinion-who actually likes being a coal miner and takes a good deal of pride in the job.

The dangers of the deep have never bothered my son, Will, but he is a hard-headed sort, not sensitive like his old man. Some have tried to persuade him to go away to Ontario, or the west, but he says he likes the pit, likes the area, and asks me why should he be forced to leave his homeland because governments will not provide jobs.

I cannot argue with him, but I know that the real reason is Ann Pyke. He says that he will go on welfare before he goes away to work and if he does he will be joining hundreds of others. There aren't many today who are hungry around here, but, as bad as welfare is, had we miners and radicals not fought tooth and nail for it in years gone by, literally thousands would have starved to death.

Will also asks me why should he go to Toronto and wait on tables in a greasy spoon when he can do a man's job in the pit. I do not have the answers so I let him go his own way.

They say that coal miners are a unique breed, that they are similar all over the world, that coal in the blood (mixed with a quantity of liquor, of course) sets men apart from their fellows. I believe it. I have been to Pennsylvania, West Virginia, and to South Wales, where centuries of death, work, and misery of all descriptions produced mining people so like Cape Bretoners that I felt instantly at home. The Welsh can sing better than us, but I would hate to predict who would win a drinking contest.

I have often wondered if everybody thinks they are unique, but I know that we do. I think I can be more objective than most because I travelled a bit more than most, and I still think that coal miners are special. It is almost as if the miserable black stuff somehow produces the greatest heroes, the foulest villains, the saddest tragedies, the happiest triumphs.

Possibly it is the very physical bleakness of a mining community which exaggerates depression and, by tremendous contrast, heightens gaiety and celebration. Parties seemed more boisterous at home than they did away and death seemed more severe, stark, and significant. Perhaps mining, with its hazards and hardships, prompts men and women to be more reckless, more colourful and, for a town of the size and population of ours, it certainly seems that more bizarre events and more startling characters have been recorded here than in rural or metropolitan areas.

Still and all, Marg has been good to me, there's no denying that. She has certainly put up with a lot of foolishness; like my drinking in younger days, when I didn't know any better, didn't care, or didn't think; like my taking off for months at a time; and like my general stubbornness and cranky nature. It cannot have been easy for her and, while I cannot say she bore it all with a smile, the times when she did blow her top and throw a plate at me were times when others would have taken a gun to me.

Above all, Marg has been a good mother to our children who, although I always loved them with a passion, often had no father to come to for help, comfort, or guidance because he was on a ship, in a union hall, or drunk in a cheap hotel.

Oh, the memories and how they come crowding back! When I was a spritely sprig of a laddybuck, who knew more than I know now because I knew everything, we lived in shacks on the edge of the world and struggled in holes in the ground. We knew about trips to the country in summertime, the rare visits to Sydney, and we knew about kicking a can down the rows and over into the sea. My world, ugly and beautiful as it was to me then, comes drifting back with little prompting- sharp contrasts: misery and cruelty, flights of joy. Though our town and our skies were grey, our life was coal black and sunshine yellow. And how I remember the soft, sunny island in the middle of the Bras d'Or lakes where I met Jeanette, that lovely, gentle woman whose soft hands will stay with me till the grave.

Of course, my mind wanders to lobsters, hot and pink from the pot; hot, dirty feet trailing in the cool waters of the June Mira; fresh, clean air and hot, new buns from Nan's country kitchen. Those things, delicious and soft to remember, take their place alongside coal, church, booze, strikes, and politics. It all takes some figuring, especially when you're old and you don't know what to do.

So I came down here to try to sort it all out in my mind and figure out why, when we worked so hard, drank so hard, and fought so hard, things did not change more than they have.

Daddy had the theory of what he called the "Trap," and I think there is a lot in the idea. We were all, so Daddy said, caught in a gigantic black trap whose huge interlocking jaws, once closed, left only tiny openings of daylight through which only the most intrepid or the most desperate managed to crawl. Those who did get out usually returned, and the majority of the toiling, troubled people scarcely had time to even look at the cracks of daylight, let alone go through them. Some, like myself, went through many times, wandered abroad and made and lost relative fortunes in other places, but always limped back, pockets empty, nursing wounds of pride, loneliness, and heartache inflicted by the cities of men.

The operators of the Trap stood alert and loud and black, towering over the levers, exhorting, berating, cajoling, threatening. The dark-suited company officials, with vest and watch-chain, raspingly urged more work, less pay, and longer hours. The black-gowned church railed against liquor, screamed against work stoppages, and convulsed at the mention of a new political order. They thumped the good black book as they asked for more money, and waved it in the air to exorcise the evil spirits of trade unionism, bolshevism, bigamy, atheism, alcoholism, rapine, plunder, and strong language. The black-frock-coated politicians, with their shiny hats and cars and starched collars, now wheedling, now thundering, told us we never had it so good, that times were bad, that times would be better, that times would get worse, depending upon whether we were being addressed by the "smug, corrupt, and aging administration" or by the "party of ideas, energy, and concern." They were booed, cheered, pelted with rocks, showered with bouquets, and went back to Halifax and Ottawa leaving us not one whit different from the way we were before they came.

The Trap has changed over the years chiefly because the operators got smarter and much more subtle. Instead of grinding the levers they began to oil them and slip them into gear quietly, gently. To be sure, the Trap opened up a lot more, and many left for fates elsewhere. Many more remained until they were guided into the cold-as-grey earth. Of course, things are better. There is still poverty, but not as much fear. The old attitudes of the church have changed, with many of the clergy now taking leading positions in activities which previously they denounced. In days gone by, people couldn't escape, now they don't want to.

Less and less it is the Trap that keeps us here, more and more it is because we have grown to love our adversity and the communities in which we have experienced it all the days of our lives.

It is the physical change I notice most. Mines flattened, buildings derelict, houses torn or burned down. The obituary column. There are no more Indians up on Raines Road, and, what is more, there are not many of us who can remember seeing them huddled together in the foulest of weathers, eking out a bare existence from the woods and the shore.

Daddy used to take me up there when he was cutting wood for his boat, for it was heavily forested then, and we would pass by dozens of families shuffling about and eating scraps. I cannot recall when they disappeared but they either died or wandered off, for there is not the slightest trace of them today

I remember Daddy showing me the old fired mines when I was just a little fellow, hoisting me on his bony shoulders, lugging me out onto the windy cliffs, and dragging me down the treacherous shale to the gaping holes overlooking the sea. They have been gone for thirty years; the coal company sealed them off with big steel doors, then pushed the earth and rocks on top. Daddy told me the French dug those mines and fired them when the English besieged Louisbourg, but that when men went into them a hundred and fifty years later they found timbers still in place and a lovely face of coal ready to be worked. One man told me he found an old pan shovel down there, which he used in his yard for years, but I have my doubts about that one.

The fired mines are just about a quarter of a mile from here, around that sandy point where the rust-red rocks stick up into the sky and kids throw stuff down, trying to start an avalanche.

One thing I always liked about living by the sea was the ease with which I could scramble down the cliff, past the alternating layers of coal and shale, and down to the pebbles. Scoop out a damp hollow for my rear end, reach out for a handful of flat stones, and sit quietly skimming them over the water. Sometimes I would lean over backwards and look upside-down like at the overhanging pillars of earth and rock and marvel at the boxy company houses precariously perched on the edges.

They called this neighbourhood the "Dump" because for more years than I can remember the coal company tipped the stone from "A" colliery onto this little beach, and to this day the rusty old railroad tracks extend about ten feet over the edge, just jutting out into nothing, waiting for some youngsters to get up to no good with them. It is indeed a wonder that one night when we were in our cups we did not trundle an old coal car over the edge.

As nice as it is to sit here, the Dump never was any garden of roses. In times past it was a brawling, gusty cauldron of bootleggers, screaming kids, loose-living women-and men, drunken carousers, immigrants who couldn't say more than "cigarette," men and boys looking for a fight-and steadily rotting old houses thrown together for the company slaves. If we have had a little more noise and a little more colour than other areas, we also had more wind. It whistled and stormed through the rows, chilling the bones and hysterically seizing the smoke from the chimneys and scattering it into the grey sky. Several times it tore roofs off the houses and carried them out to sea. Once, ours went, and Daddy kidded me that it had sailed clear to Newfoundland, but we found it about thirty feet from here, crumpled up on the rocks.

Although I often came down here I never swam in this water. Today, a fellow could do it without any problem because they stopped dumping here some years ago, and it was the dumping made the water so filthy. Lord, it was black! A little fellow would have to build coal castles! There wasn't much sand in those days and what little you could find was a dark-grey, gritty substance, which clung to your skin and sent shivers up your spine.

No, when I wanted to go swimming there were far better places than Dump beach, places clean and cool, exciting and secret, where a boy could hide from the world of men by sliding under the huge rocks and lying there with his cheek against the cold, green stone. I remember swimming off the sand bar when they held open air meetings down there. It was one of the few places that could accommodate several hundred men without interference from the company or police.

Jim MacLachlan would be standing on an old wagon, waving his long arms and shouting about the capitalist system while hundreds of miners stood rapt, only occasionally shifting their weight from one foot to the other or stifling the odd cough. Daddy and my older brothers would be there, standing erect, shoulder to shoulder, straining for every word, as if they were pure gold.

Later, I was the same, pit boots planted firmly in the sand, wind wrapping my hair across my face, and my eyes glued to the tall figure whose power of oratory conjured up the denizens of hell, and then dispelled them with visions of a society without want, without fear, and without war.

That was later; at first I had no idea what was going on, and if they were revolting in Russia it made no difference to me. Bored with the speeches, we young fellows would slip away through the lanky legs, hide our clothes under a pile of stones, and wade into the sea. Lonnie MacLaren would stand waist deep, waving his arms in mockery: "Workers unite! Down with capitalism!" until the rest of us got to him and dragged him down.

Then we'd get dressed and sneak back, me sidling up to Daddy's long, thin frame, head cocked to one side as though intent on the proceedings and had been there the whole time. If he ever caught on he never mentioned it.

When Jim had finished calling down the company, the government, and all the stars in the sky, he'd put his teeth back into his mouth and scramble down from the wagon. My father, eyes glazed with admiration and hope, would sniff, rub the back of his hairy hand under his nose, and look down, grabbing me by the back of the neck. "Well, Donnie Ross," he'd ask, his eyes steel blue and clear as a country brook, "did you hear what the man said?"

"Yes, Daddy."

"Good. You remember it, b'y, and some day you'll understand what it all means."

"Yes, Daddy," I'd say automatically, tugging at his pants and anxious to be away home for supper.

"All right, b'y, home with us. Your mother's got codfish."

And off we'd go, Daddy taking huge strides, his heavy black boots pounding in the sand, and me running along for all the world like a little dog. We would pause briefly at the bridge and peer down into the black current below.

Normally I did not bother Daddy when he was hanging over the bridge rail since, even at that age, it occurred to me that when he was thinking he would not want to be disturbed by foolish questions. One day, however, I asked, "Daddy, what's a capitalist?"

"A capitalist..." he mused, inclining his head and pondering the question as if it was perfectly usual from a child of my age, "is a man who takes from the people what is not his but theirs." He nodded sagely, pleased with the profundity of his reply, but felt compelled to add, "Kind of a thief, in a way."

"You mean like Lazy Jackie?" I asked, remembering how that shabby individual sneaked along our picket fence and stole a bundle of kindling from our yard.

"No, no, b'y," he gestured emphatically in my face with his stubs of fingers so I could see the blue marks where the doctors had sewn the skin over the bits of bone. "'Lazy Jackie is nothing but an ignorant wretch who never had no opportunity to know which end was up. And don't be fooled by folks calling him lazy. He's a product of his environment."

"What's environment, Daddy?".

"'You're after asking too many questions, b'y, but since you ask, I'll tell you that there are some men, big and strong to the eye, who can no more do a day's work with a pan shovel than fly to the moon because their bones are soft, their lungs are black, and their minds are weak."

"Is the company a capitalist?" I asked, determined to get to the bottom of the mystery.

"Are you ever smart! The company is owned by capitalists who take the cream of our coal and the life's blood of our people and do not so much as build a park bench or plant a tree in return!"

I summoned up the pictures from the *Record* in my mind's eye and saw company officials with their black three-piece suits, watch-chains, wing-tip collars, and cold, staring, beady eyes. I felt obliged to hate them because I was sure Daddy did. "Do you hate the capitalists, Daddy?"

"'I hate no one, b'y," he said very softly, straightening up and rubbing his elbows. "I only pity the lackeys of the system because they are slaves to it as well as masters of it."

I felt no urge to have this clarified, even though I did not understand it, because it was uttered with such authority I felt it would be saucy to require further comment. Instead I kicked a stone into the brook, tugged at Daddy's coat, and started away up the road.

And many's the time around about dusk a tall, thin man in a tattered coat, a small urchin running around his legs, could be seen coming up from the sand bar, over the bridge, across the railroad tracks, and down into the Dump to a waiting supper and an anxious woman.

My father was a strange man. At the age of six he came with his widowed father from Newfoundland. He went into the pit when he was ten, and stayed there until he was seventy-one, in later years being shunted to the surface to sweep the wash-house or tend the lamps, for there were no pensions for anyone who was not an official. My father was offered the overman's job on scores of occasions, but he always refused saying—in my opinion, quite wrongly

—that an overman was next to a pimp. He worked in seven collieries in his sixty-one gnarled and brow-beaten years with the company, and was in more strikes and stoppages than he had fingers on both hands; he went through more election campaigns—the Independent Labour Party, and the Communist Party—than Johnny the Dog had hot dinners.

In the thirties, he was reluctantly drawn into the C.C.F., but against his better judgment because he thought it wishy-washy. He ran for the I.L.P. nomination one election and was beaten out by five votes; the man to whom he lost the nomination was beaten at the polls by over five thousand. On such occasions he would shake his head, sighing with a mixture of anger and pity, and blasphemously say to nobody in particular, "Forgive them for they know not what they do."

My father was the kind of man who was able to be stern and gentle at the same time, and I rarely saw him harm a living soul, leastways without cause. Seldom even in the hectic emotional moments of a strike would he be violent, and many times in the local union he would be shouted down for being too soft.

One man, a roary-eyed immigrant, with rum on his breath and a nagging wife at home, used to rise time after time to scream, "Burn the church! Kill the priest! Strike! Strike!" My father would rise slowly, holding out one scarred hand towards the platform the other towards the offender, throw back his head, and fix his eyes on the United Mineworkers insignia above the table. "Brother chairman," he would boom, "times are bringing us troubles enough, but the idiocy of Brother Potovsk only exacerbates the situation."

The first time he used the word, the men laughed because they thought he was putting on the dog, but later they got used to the language picked up from the magazines and leftwing newspapers, which came in the mail from Chicago, and became quite proud of it. "Educated Tom," they called him, although he had virtually no formal learning, and his use of big words ensured that he was never really popular.

Daddy often said that he did not want to be liked as long as he was respected. That he received respect from his fellow unionists was evidenced by his repeated election to various committees and convention delegations, chiefly one suspects so their press statements would come out full of high-sounding expressions and complex phrases.

One such statement, put out by him when he was chairman of the press committee, was a classic, and I still have it up in the attic. It was in 1919, when Woodsworth and others were charged with seditious libel during the Winnipeg General Strike, and a motion was carried on the floor instructing Brother Ross to draft a suitable resolution. He withdrew briefly, sucking on his blackened briar pipe, and sauntered back with the proposed draft in his hand. Before speaking, my father struck up a semi-theatrical pose, rubbed his nose, fingered his moustache, removed his pipe, and loudly cleared his throat. "Whereas the perfidious, dastardly and unjustified actions of the authorities in incarcerating Brother Woodsworth and his esteemed colleagues has violated the fundamental rights of mankind, be it resolved that this local union vehemently protests such insidious betrayal of human dignity and categorically demands the immediate release of these fine men before the flagrant treachery exacerbates the already inflammatory situation."

They loved it! It was carried unanimously amid a chorus of cheers, which was followed by a vote of thanks for his efforts. My father was very proud of the resolution and was beside himself with rage when the local newspaper did not print it in its entirety. There was nothing he could do except curse the publisher and editor as lackeys of the capitalist system and vow never again to submit his releases to the paper. He did not carry out his threat, but it made him feel better at the time.

The single occasion on which my father did get violent was when Danny Ginger MacRae, a company official, called Reverend Swain a murderer. Danny Ginger had been put out to pasture by the coal company when he had lost an arm in a fall. He was a gross, surly man, more concerned with ill-treating men than production while he was working, and more concerned with his consumption of liquor than the welfare of his family while on pension. He invariably spent his days in the tavern and that was where my father thrashed him. Not that Daddy drank much, but he often went into the tavern to distribute literature.

Daddy was carefully making his way around the battered tables, waving away the thick smoke with his hand, and laying the political tracts in front of the grumbling, reticent drinkers, when he overheard the offensive remark. He whirled around, his eyes blazing, his fist clenched.

"Daniel MacRae," he bellowed, "as God is my witness, you're a damned liar! Reverend Swain was one of the finest men who ever drew breath, and to call him a murderer is to blaspheme!"

"Tom Ross, you're a fool," Ginger sneered over his ale. "Swain was a bolshevik and bolsheviks is murderers."

"Reverend Swain was one of the best friends that working people ever had and, by God, you'll retract that statement!"

"Never!" Danny Ginger spat. "All bolsheviks and socialists is murderers and always will be."

"John Francis," my father called to a man seated at a nearby table. "Off with your belt and tie my arm behind my back so it will not be said I took advantage of a disabled man."

They stuck his right arm inside the back of his big, black belt and tied it there with John Francis's brown one and let him go.

Danny Ginger was hardly out of his chair when my father was on top of him, pounding his face with the half-fist left on his arm. They reached down and pulled the great, drooling lump of a man to the little back door and dragged him out among the trash cans in the yard.

John Francis hastily propelled my still raving father out of the front door and down the street before the police arrived. When Sergeant MacAdam asked what had been going on, Piggy Clements told him that the stain on the floor was the blood of the martyrs of the revolution, and that it would never dry as long as coal was mined in the town.

Neither Daddy nor Danny Ginger was caught, but Piggy Clements was locked up for the night and John Francis was ordered to clean up the blood.

2: Drinking heaven dry

I saw near to fifty thousand men, women, and children brought to the verge of starvation in these coalfields during the 1925 strike, the longest and most bitter on record, and after it was over many wasted away from tuberculosis, calcium deficiencies, and generally rotten diets. My good friend Dr. Singh says I'm being sentimental and don't know what I'm talking about, but I know more about medicine than he thinks and I certainly know more than he does about the pit and what it can do to a man.

We have a good old chewing of the fat, the Doc and I, and when he says I'm trying to make poetry out of everyday life and death, I tell him he's case-hardened and is the product of a society and a sub-continent where life is cheap.

Over the years I have seen men from the Dump here dropping dead at ages thirty and forty because their lungs could not absorb more coal dust or diesel fumes or their hearts and their backs just got weary of shovelling and mucking behind the miner for so long. I am very thankful I shall not die in the wash-house, or on the rake, or at the wall; I'll die in my bed or in the tavern, not in the evil, black hole.

When I was a little boy it seemed that there was never enough to eat; not that I remember being continually hungry, but that there wasn't enough. Apart from supper, when we often had codfish and potatoes, meals seemed to consist of scraps, leftovers from the previous day's main meal, with bread and some little thing added to make it interesting.

Ma always tried to give my father something decent, but often that was only bits of dried cod with dripping fat. Often I would come in from hanging about the cliffs or getting coal from the beach and ask my mother for a snack, but she would tell me to wait until Daddy got home from work.

It was like an eternity waiting for the sound of his big pit boots to come scraping over the step. He would push open the door, peer in, almost as if he expected to find himself in another house, throw his old cap on the dresser, and heave himself into the old rocker with a long, tired, tearful sigh. He would rub his red eyes with his hands, displaying the black lines around his fingernails, pull off his scarf, which made a soft, rasping noise as it ran over his dry, leathery neck, straighten up, and call for his food.

Then we would eat. My father would say grace in his own peculiar fashion much disliked by Ma and Father Angus: "Lord, keep us ever mindful of the struggles of our own classes the world over and help us look forward to the day when men of all origins will be able to enjoy food in abundance, shelter aplenty, work without begging for it, and freedom to express themselves and be heard in the councils of the nations of the world."

He always crossed himself before and after, but Ma still said it was too much like a Protestant grace for her liking.

He sniffed and ate.

I was born at the turbulent turn of the century, during one of the earliest strikes, so it must have been a terrible struggle for Ma with no pay coming in and my sister, my two older brothers, and me, a bawling infant demanding milk and attention. Despite what now seems to me desperate living conditions, our family did not fare as badly as others did, partly due to fate, partly to my mother's thrift and inventiveness, and my father's sobriety. At the time, apparently, the family owed nothing to the company —our rent, coal, church, doctor, company store, carbide, and powder all checked off and up to date— and Daddy had managed, God knows how, to put a few dollars away in the old tea can on the kitchen shelf.

Others were not nearly as fortunate: one woman, eight months pregnant, was kicked and beaten and thrown with her dirty mattress into the snowy street; a miner who owed back rent was herded out of his house with nineteen children and an ailing wife.

Those who owed the company were often men who had lost time through sickness and could not catch up. As a result they might be indebted to the company for the rest of their lives, and some men— from the day they went to work to the day they died

—never knew what it was to hold any actual money in their hands. On one pay-day, the famous story goes, a MacDonald man drew one cent, and ever since that far-off day the family has been known as the Big Pays.

Even when times were cruel the miners had a sense of humour, and it was just as well, for many would have gone mad without it.

The interminable battle for better conditions went on year after year and, to a lesser extent, is still going on. Conditions the miners take for granted today were gained through long, drawn-out, vicious fights, which erupted and re-erupted until finally, through force of arms and sheer stubbornness, we dragged the company, kicking and screaming, down the rocky road of industrial safety.

Even today, governments and company officials will not admit to things which I, in my heart, know to be true. I remember men fired for fouling the washhouse floor while they were in the showers. I tried to tell both union and company that molasses and potatoes and twenty years of working behind the miner, and some men didn't know when their bowels were moving, but they would not listen.

Men died in other ways too: around this town many drank themselves to death. First liquor, and when they could not afford the real stuff, rubbing alcohol, shaving lotion, vanilla, and anything else they could get their hands on.

They can be seen today, as they could be in years gone by, stumbling and lolling around Senator's

Corners in Glace Bay, hunched on the steps of the tavern or post office, or staggering up the row in the sodden twilight of their depressing, bleary existence. Men melted shoe polish and strained molten gramophone records through a loaf of bread, eagerly slobbering over the foul liquid which gathered in an old can or a chipped saucer.

A friend of my father's told me Little Angus MacIsaac and Tommy Daley used to make the stuff down in Tommy's squalid shack by the wharf, and the sticky, heavy smell would attract birds of a feather to go stumbling in and listen to music while they drifted further into the painless, foggy fellowship from which very few returned unscathed.

One night Tommy asked Red Dan MacInnis to play his favourite record, but none of them could find it. Tommy blundered around the dark, evil-smelling shack searching desperately until he stopped by the bubbling pot. He reached in and pulled out a drooping, tarry label and, head cocked to one side, examined it closely. He let out a screech which was heard a block away, seized Old Billy MacNeil's stick, and pitched into Little Angus with a fanatical passion.

He chased him out of the shack and down along the shore shouting, "You no good sonofabitch, I'll break your jeez legs, you just drank me 'Black Velvet Band!'"

They say that Cape Bretoners are drinking heaven dry and it may be true because there were hundreds like myself who drank for pure pleasure. However, miners drank for a variety of reasons, none of them very savoury. Some men knew that they would never have anything, knew they'd spend their whole lives covered in coal and living in shacks, so they drank to make the coal more tolerable and the shacks more comfortable. Others drank to ease the pain in their legs and arms where the damp, hot-cold levels had given them rheumatism and arthritis. Still others would tell you, between gasps and wheezes, that they drank to help them breathe easier. Stumpy Allan MacSwain had the best reason: "Because it won't do me any harm."

There's a great deal to be said for a long, cool golden draft, especially on a summer's evening after a hard day in the pit. Tilting the tall glass back and gazing down in the pale amber glow would set a man's mind going in a thousand different directions, momentarily bestowing total comprehension, genius, and super-strength. The good froth would splash gently into your nose, just like the ocean at Burke's Point, and when you put the empty glass back on the table with a solid, satisfying thump, you were like a diver coming up for air.

There would be all the fellows, exactly as you left them, red in the face, eyes bright, lips glistening, all friends. A toothy grin, a belch of gratitude for all God's good gifts, a deep breath, and a loud, hearty call for another.

There's no harm in drinking, in my opinion, if you only hurt yourself, but when you hurt your family then the drink is the devil. The Sally Ann, the Temperance Band, and all the other well-wishing, starch-stiff, righteous uprights all proclaimed that drink was the curse of the working classes, but from the details they gave of cirrhosis of the liver, heart disease, blood disorder, and the relegation of the imbiber to the very fires of hell, I imagined it was a curse to other classes as well, but they were never mentioned. Apparently, the pit manager snuffling his scotch whisky behind a filing cabinet, or the mine owner sodden with brandy at his Sunday dinner table, or the president of the board tight with champagne in a London hotel, were all merely enjoying the entitled relief from the heavy responsibilities of office. In no way were they cursed, for it was to them that we owed our bread, our very lives.

As Father Angus preached it, "Were it not for the company, you would all starve!" Rummy Alfie LeBlanc replied out loud that if it had not been for the company most of us would not be here. Father Angus, naturally, gave him a terrible holy tongue-lashing, as indeed he did to Johnny Boxer, who got drunk aboard a Spanish freighter and woke up in the mid-Atlantic.

Liquor made some men saints, some maniacs, some pitiful, snivelling mice, but mostly it just filled miners with devilish fun and unbounded energy. Once I went to Glace Bay with Archie Chisholm and we met up with Mickey A. MacLean outside the Legion in New Aberdeen. As night fell, and we got more into us, Archie began to get belligerent, and each statement was uttered with the authority and pomposity of a Papal bull.

Mickey A., contrary as always, took strong objection to this pattern and relentlessly argued everything Archie said. By ten o'clock they were ready to murder each other and I, in my light-headed state, could do nothing to mediate the situation nor, I think, did I want to, for I was enjoying the performance.

Finally, Archie jumped up, crashing his glass to the table. "I can fight you," he yelled, "and put the biggest beatin' on you that yous ever had!"

"Is that right?" Mickey A. rose slowly, cracking his huge knuckles. "Why you son of a Newfoundlander, I'll tear you to pieces!"

"Outside!" Archie yelled, making for the door. "Outside it is!"

I did not even try to protest because I knew it would do no good, and I relaxed myself and prepared for a donnybrook. They started fighting right on the street outside the Legion and an hour and a half later we were down in the Sterling, still swinging and swearing.

At half after midnight, we had reached Caledonia and Archie and Mickey A. collapsed into a drain alongside the school. I slumped down beside them, almost as out of breath from refereeing as they were from fighting

Archie turned to Mickey A. "You're a fine fighter, Mickey, b'y. What do you say we call it a tie?"

"Okay, Archie," he gasped. "I reckon we're evenly matched."

"'I wouldn't say that," Archie said seriously. "After all, my punches are straighter than yours."

"Straighter, are they?" shouted Mickey A., getting up from the roadside. "I'll show you whose punches are straight, bejesus!"

And at it they went again, yelling and pounding like two tomcats clawing over a cat in heat. In Passchendaele they fell, helplessly over a fence, hardly having the strength to wipe the drool from their faces. The words, what few there were now, came out one by one, hoarsely, haltingly.

"I...can...beat...you, you...bastard."

"No...you...can't...you sonofabitch..."

At three-thirty in the morning we found ourselves out on the Sydney Road, Archie and Mickey A. locked in a weird, shambling embrace, and me tottering behind wondering how in the world I had got into that situation.

When finally they dropped, senseless, I woke up a buddy of mine who lived nearby and together we dragged them inside and covered them over with a blanket.

As I huddled over a cup of hot tea, Archie stirred in his sleep and muttered softly, "I'll beat you, I'll beat you, I'll..."

Another time I was out drinking with my brother Tom and Harold Nearing. Walking along together, they made a strange sight: Tom, six-feet-four and a hundred and ninety pounds, Harold five-feet-six, weighing about a hundred and twenty. Despite his size, Harold could be vicious and mean, and a night

in our cups invariably meant his getting cantanker-
ous somewhere along the line.

We had drunk all our money and were sniffing
around the rows for someone to touch for a loan. It
was a steamy, inhospitable night, but eventually we
ran Freddie MacDonald to ground and, more by
threat of force than anything else, managed to
squeeze out of him a dirty, crumpled five-dollar bill.

It was a godsend; with that we could go to a bootlegger and drink for another hour—but something
happened. To this day, I don't know what did it, but
quite suddenly Harold grabbed the bill and tore it
into a thousand pieces.

Tom went berserk, screeching and jumping up
and down, his arms flailing like a windmill. He
cursed and abused Harold, his mother, father, and all
his family, mouthing the foulest obscenities he could
bring to his inflamed tongue. Harold made the fatal
mistake of laughing and Tom laid the most terrible
beating on him I have ever seen.

Feeling guilty for what had happened the night
before, I went over to Harold's house to see how he
was. He was bruised, cut, and bandaged from head
to foot, and lay on the sofa moaning softly. His wife, a
big garrulous woman, was standing over him demanding to know who had beaten him, but Harold,
thinking I would carry the message to Tom if he told
the truth, kept silent. Mrs. Nearing was getting more
belligerent by the minute and, by standing over him
like a great bulldog, she threatened to give him more
of the same if he didn't confess immediately.

Harold panicked. He hoisted himself up onto the back of the sofa, wildly looking about him as though some object in the room would give him inspiration. His wife began to roll up her sleeves and move forward for the kill, when suddenly there was a tap at the door and in walked Teddy McIntyre from across the street.

Desperately frightened, still sore from the last beating, and at his wit's end, Harold became hysterical. "He did it!" Harold shouted, pointing at Teddy. "He's the one you want, old woman!"

"'S-o-o-o!" Mrs. Nearing turned on the amazed Teddy. "Beat up my old man, would you? I'll show you a thing or two, my laddybuck!"

Teddy cowered against the door, shaking his head in bewilderment as Mrs. Nearing laid into him with a vengeance. Teddy gibbered with disbelief, looking from Harold to me, trying to read an explanation in our faces as he warded off the raining blows.

I lost control and fell to the floor convulsed with laughter while Harold, now standing up on the bouncing sofa, waved his arms and urged his wife on to victory.

"Whatever it is, I didn't do it!" Teddy protested, first bellowing, then whining, "Honest, Missiz, I didn't do it!"

"Don't listen to him, Mary," Harold screamed. "Kill him, he's the one!"

At last, unable to bear it any longer, and convinced he would not find out the reason from the irate woman, a screaming maniac covered in bandages or a giggling fool rolling about on the carpet, Teddy grabbed the door and tore out into the street. In a flurry of dogs, children, and squawking chickens, Mrs. Nearing flew after him and chased him to the tenth row where she ran out of breath and curses.

Harold and I beat it out of the back door and took off for the tavern.

Half of the fun in drinking in those days was in keeping enough booze money out of the wife's clutches, for almost every one of them would search their husband's pockets after they were asleep. Men would go to any lengths and tell the most outlandish lies in order to keep a little cash to spend on liquor. Some men invented special rates of pay, lower than the datal rate, and for decades, wives would not know that ten per cent of the wages was retained for alcoholic pursuits.

Billy Tickle Arse told his simple wife he was a stone-taster, the lowest paid job in the colliery. In company he would encourage his friends to enlarge on this occupation, and seeing his cheery wink, we obliged by explaining how none of us would want the task of licking rock to see if it was "pure." He would even hang out his red, leathery tongue and ask innocently if anyone had ever seen such a rough and worn specimen; we all shook our heads solemnly and swore we had not.

Whenever a contract vote was coming up, Billy would chuckle, cluck his tongue, and say, "Good contract, but no raise for the stone-tasters again."

I will never forget the time Tom the Fiddler hid

his benefit cheque from his wife when they refused to cash it at the tavern. Apparently, Fiddler had bounced a few cheques on them and they had instructions to be very wary of him.

In spite of the ruckus he raised, Walter Penney, the bartender, was adamant; Fiddler would have to cash it at the bank, but the bank was closed for the day. He managed to borrow the money from my brother Tom with the solemn oath that he would cash the cheque first thing in the morning and repay him.

That night, Fiddler hunted desperately for a new hiding place, his wife having discovered most of his habitual ones, and finally hit on the outhouse. He ducked inside the danksmelling little hut and reached up, placing the cheque on the ledge over the doorway. He stooped, picked up a tiny pebble, laid it on the cheque, and went into the house bloated with beer and gleeful in his deceit.

The next day was full of breeze, blarney, birds, and high skies, but when Fiddler reached the rickety old outhouse his rejoicing rapidly left him. The cheque was gone.

I was strolling up the row at I the time and I heard Fiddler hissing to me over the fence.

"Psst! Come here quick, Donnie!"

"What is it, Fiddler?"

"'Shsst, not so loud. A catastrophe has befallen the Fiddler in his hour of direst need."

I felt above the ledge and even stood on the seat to look, but the cheque was well and truly gone.

When I verified this fact to Fiddler, he was distraught.

"With his godawful temper, your brother will kill me if I don't pay him back today," he said woefully, and I could not deny it.

I shifted the wad of chewing tobacco in my mouth and leaned over the malodorous hole to spit. The mucus stayed on my tongue as I stared into the sordid, gaping opening.

There was the cheque, lying neatly on top of the refuse of a hundred dinners, a great, ugly black fly perched on it.

I gagged as I clutched Fiddler's shirtsleeve and pointed silently downwards.

Despite the circumstances, Fiddler was so relieved to find the cheque he didn't bat an eyelid. He fished a piece of newspaper out of a cardboard box on the floor and with a deep breath dived and came up with a crumpled bundle.

"Get the b'ys," said Fiddler resolutely as he stuffed obscene shape into his pants pocket. "I'm not going to be cheated out of my money now."

The bank manager was a tiny, dowdy, frightened man wearing an ill-fitting three-piece suit and gold-rimmed spectacles perched on the end of his button nose. He had a hole-in-the-heart son, a domineering wife, and a hawk-like superior; it all showed in his face and his manner. His name was Pyge, but Fiddler pronounced it "pig."

We had ambled downtown, all but two of us ignorant of the ramifications of the mission on which we were embarked, and all along the way the other men were sniffing the air and peering down at their boots.

We gathered around the little gap in the wiremesh fence which kept the cashiers from being grabbed by would-be bank robbers, and propelled Fiddler forward through our ranks.

"Mr. Pig," he said seriously, "I have a cheque I want you to cash for me."

"Certainly, Mr. MacEachern." Pyge blinked rapidly through the thick lenses and smiled insipidly.

Fiddler dug his hand into his pocket, pulled out the paper ball, and, at arm's length, slowly unwrapped it to reveal the soiled cheque with the fly, now dead, still sitting on it.

The boys groaned with disgust then doubled up, turned away, and spluttered with mirth, weird noises like whining buzz saws coming from their stifled faces.

Mr. Pyge turned white, then—I swear it—green. His mouth opened and a silent protest formed on his lips, but when Fiddler's huge, hairy fist was held gently in front of him, the slight shake of his head changed to a reluctant nod.

"Just wash it off under the tap, Mr. Pig," said Fiddler, very businesslike. "It's as good as gold, and a little honest dirt won't hurt you."

"How much is it for?" Pyge whispered, not daring to look.

"Five dollars, Mr. Pig," Fiddler said pompously. "No more, no less. You have my word as a gentleman."

Outside on the sidewalk, the money clutched in my brother's hand, we exploded, falling over each other, helpless as babies, as the daily bustling life of the town looked on with raised eyebrows. Seated boisterously around the tavern table we raised our glasses and Fiddler intoned an impromptu toast to the free enterprise banking system.

3: Pure as a mountain stream

Marg never minded the odd times when I came home feeling good, but my mother acted as if one drop was a spear driven into her old heart. Sometime before I was married, I had come back from Hamilton with my pockets full of money, a yearning to see old friends and familiar places, and a powerful thirst. I landed in drunk and I stayed that way for three whole days.

Ma was mortified and one morning, a few days before Christmas, she crept into the tiny bedroom and sat on the edge of the white quilted bed.

I had a head like a drum and it felt as if there was a fellow wearing pit boots tramping about on my tongue. I turned over painfully, squinted against the searing light, and peered up at her wrinkled brown face. "What!" I was cranky as the devil.

"'Donnie, b'y," she cooed softly, but it sounded like a shot firer blasting his charge behind my ear, "I want you to promise your Ma something."

"Wassat?"

"Promise your Ma you'll go to confession tomorrow and then stay sober over Christmas Day."

"All right," I muttered, more to get rid of her than

anything else, and she went out with a smile on her face.

Being an eminently practical man, I knew I had one day left for freedom before my rash promise went into effect, so when I met Willie Norman MacLean in Glace Bay at noontime, I decided to have one last final fling. We ended up late that night rolling in the ditches in Number Eleven.

Although I was not supposed to start carrying out the pledge until the next day, I thought it wise not to go home, so I stayed in a place I would not reveal to anyone in my family and to few of my friends.

In view of the fact that Ma had not specified what time of day, when I awoke at midday, I reasoned that a small hair of the dog would put me in a better frame of mind to face confession, so Willie Norman and I went to his uncle's house and stayed until dark, drinking Newfoundland Screech.

Feeling full of remorse, I left Willie Norman's uncle's about five o'clock and made my way to church. Naturally I did not tell Father Angus everything—not wishing to offend his delicate sensibilit- ies—but enough to keep him in gossip for a few days.

When I was just through the big oak doors I brushed up against a man who was standing on the steps looking out over the bay.

"'Donnie Ross, that you?" he asked, peering through the gathering gloom.

"'Lardjeez, Spooner MacIntyre. What in the world are you doing perched on the church steps at this time of night?"

"Purging my soul," he said wickedly, and breathed into my face.

Now, some people will tell you that the smell of secondhand liquor is a foul thing to behold, but I never found that to be the case. Even second hand, the good, strong fumes of rum started to stir my insides and I rubbed my hand over my face and looked both ways.

"You've been to a party, Spooner," I said.

"'I have not."

"Then you've been eating Christmas pudding with rum sauce."

"As a matter of fact, Donnie Ross," he said with a sly grin, "I'm after having a little something on my hip."

"'Is that right?"

"It is," he said, smiling. "Could I persuade you to join me in a little drop to keep out the cold?"

That the weather was freezing and inhospitable nobody could deny, and I never let it be said of me that I was an unsociable man. Here was a good stout friend wishing me the best of the festive season—good will to men and peace on earth—who was I, I thought, to be throwing his comradeship back in his face?

"Well, that's very kind of you, Spooner, but only one wee nip."

"Sure."

"Just one now, Spooner."

"Sure, b'y," he said, passing over the flat little

bottle.

As I felt the harsh liquor burning my lips and trickling down to the cockles of my young heart, the clouds suddenly cleared and I realized that Ma had made me promise not to get drunk; she had said nothing about a small tot for purely social reasons.

"That's good, Spooner," I said gratefully.

"It is indeed, b'y, have another nip."

"Well, just one, Spooner, just one," said I, tipping it back and feeling that warm, welcome trickle.

I was aware of a swift movement of Spooner's arm and heard a tinkle as the empty bottle smashed on the cobbles as we turned into his dowdy company house. The interior was in marked contrast to the bleak outside and the back kitchen was a warm and inviting cocoon.

Spooner's father, John Joe MacIntyre, had shot six rabbits that day and the pot of stew was pungently simmering on the old black stove. When a big plate-ful was placed in front of me, I set into it with rare energy.

While I was sopping up the rich gravy with a bit of home-made bread, Spooner left the table and crouched under the sink. He fumbled around for a minute then emerged with a big jug of bright, clear liquid.

"Will you sample the old man's latest batch of shine?" he asked, eyes gleaming.

"Ooooh," the soft sound sprang from my evil lips as he swished it around under my nose. I sniffed the strange, almost surgical, bittersweet odour. "It is

Christmas, ain't it?"

"Indeed it is," Spooner said obligingly as he put two old chipped cups on the table and filled them half-full. "Pure as a mountain stream."

Spooner winked, walked to the stove for the blackened kettle, filled the cups to the brim with hot water, and pushed the sugarbowl across to me.

"Compliments of the season," I said with a sigh.

I can swear now, as I did then, that I did not get drunk. However, I declined to go home because it was getting late and I did not want to wake up Ma by blundering up the stairs in the dark.

Spooner's children, mischievous and snotty-nosed all, told my brothers that I did not stay at their house that night, but they were lying. In any case, they were up in bed and could not have seen me tiptoeing down the street to Sarah O'Donnell's little cottage at the end of the wind.

The next day I met Daddy struggling up the Fourth Row on his way to church and the terrible look he gave me could have frozen a Newfoundland dog to a spruce tree.

"'Your Ma is mad at you."

"At me?"

"Yes, you goddamned layabout!!"

"Daddy, harsh words for Christmas Day."

"'Yes, and more you'll get too if you don't get to church and have communion."

"'That's exactly where I was going," I said quite truthfully. "I'll walk with you."

"And you'll go straight home after?"

"Sure," I said sheepishly. "I'll meet you on the steps after mass."

"We've got a beautiful chicken for dinner," he said and started to shuffle away, me alongside.

The church was so crowded that I had to stand at the back. I could not take communion because of my promise to Father Angus, but I sang a little and felt truly repentant.

Spooner must have been back to the church before I got there because the smell of rum was still hanging in the air. It was only faint and probably came off the breath of one of the kneeling worshippers, but it was driving me mad.

Unable to stand it any longer, I crossed myself and tore out of the church and away down the street.

I went down to Neilie MacNeil, the bootlegger on Kelly Street, and bought a pint of whisky. One sip was all I wanted to fix me up so I could go home to dinner in reasonable shape. I took a small drink and stuffed the bottle into my coat pocket, thinking it might be welcome at the table after dinner.

It was a bleak, grey, bitter morning, with the flying snow like fine needle points. I stopped by the ball-park to take a little nip to keep out the dreadful cold when someone tapped me on the shoulder.

"Having a wee nip, Donnie?" It was Reggie Ryan, the policeman.

"Good day, Reggie, will you have one yourself?"

"Well," he said, easing the bottle out of my hand, "'I will take just one, for Christmas."

"Will you do me a favour?" I asked as he tipped

the whisky to his big red lips.

"Name it, b'y," he said, wiping his mouth with the back of his gloved hand.

"Will you...keep the bottle...as a Christmas gift?"

"That's right handsome of you, b'y."

"Good," I said. "I must be away."

"One moment there." Reggie sounded hurt.

"What is it?" I turned back and saw a bottle of good rum in his hand, the whisky bottle now dangling at his side. "You'll do me the honour of having a drink with me now?"

"I guess."

I took a swig, spat in the snow, lit up a cigarette, and pulled my coat around me. "Now I must go. Merry Christmas to you, Reggie."

"You forgot your gift," he said, smiling.

"My gift?"

"'Sure," said Reggie, thrusting the rum into my hand. "One gift deserves another. All the best!"

So I missed Christmas completely. I saw Ma in town a few days later and she did not speak. I went to Hamilton the next weekend so I did not speak to her again for five months.

It is, I know, a terrible thing to admit, but in some ways I am almost sorry that you don't see the kind of drinking like you used to; at least it added colour to our drab lives. At one time it was difficult to navigate Commercial Street in Glace Bay without bumping into at least twenty drunks and a dozen fights, but all that has changed.

The fighting Cape Bretoner of legend is no more;

there are some, like Georgie Lainz, who will haul off and plant you one as soon as look at you, but for the most part the people here will treat you as civilized as anyone on earth. We got soft and maybe it was liquor that did it.

Many say it is the lack of liquor and I can't make up my mind which is right.

4: The impersonal monolith

In our little town of two thousand people we have witnessed seven murders in my time, although few of them have been officially declared such. During some of the strikes the detested Pinkertons came in here and slaughtered militant union leaders up back alleys, making it look like an accident. A particularly hated company official was once viciously attacked by the women in the Fourth Row as he came home in the dark one night. His mutilated body was found in the drain, clawed and bitten from head to foot.

Dusty Malcolm killed three of his children by starving them and his wife by choking her. He then proceeded to take his fourteen-year-old daughter to bed with him and later, when she escaped to tell of her physical and mental abuse, he sent her away to Quebec.

He still lived until only a few years ago, an old wrinkled man sitting on his step, quietly smoking his pipe, smug in the knowledge that once he had powerful friends.

I can't prove it, you understand, but we all know.

Jock Anderson, the grocer, killed his own father and lived on in decadence and perversion until he was ninety-four. A huge broad-chested, rosy-faced man, Jock kicked his aged father to the floor, beat him with a whisky bottle, and then kicked him savagely about the head.

The three witnesses who stood by while the old man was sent to the promised land were ruled incompetent by the judge, who happened to be Jock's cousin.

Anderson, then sole owner of the store, proceeded to erect a massive house, which he called Bartholomew Hall, named in honour of his father. When the mansion was opened a little over a year, police raided it to find Jock obscenely molesting two small girls on the billiard table in his lavish front room.

The case never came to court and the parents of the children in question suddenly acquired shiny new cars. Again, I have no proof, but honest people swear to it.

If coal brought out the best in people—like Will MacKinnon, who married a beautiful, wealthy girl, then stepped over the fence three days after the wedding to live with an ugly, poverty-stricken widow for the rest of his life—t also brought out the worst in them.

Winnifred MacGilivray, lively and pretty as a field of corn in the wind, lay down in that field one summer's day and allowed young Freddie Boudreau to sow the seeds of the season with an abandon of youth and perspiration. When she discovered that a harvest would be forthcoming, she said not a word to Freddie, allowing him to go away to Montreal to find work, contrived to deliver herself of the unborn, and mailed it to him in a sordid, crumpled brown-paper parcel.

Numbed and revolted, Freddie Boudreau wandered in a daze down Ste. Catherine Street and was mowed down by a truck.

When she was told that her lover was dead, Winnie MacGilivray smiled and said mysteriously, "Then that makes two of them."

Instances of cruelty and inhumanity were usually associated with the coal company, which, while exaggerated in our minds to the status of an incredibly evil monster of gigantic proportions, none the less never went out of its way to show the slightest compassion no matter how severe the circumstances.

Allister MacDonnell, who operated the fan in the hell-hole, which went by the name of the Montreal Mine, worked seven shifts a week, fifty-two weeks a year; he had to, it was "company's orders." He had worked at the job for twenty-eight years and in that time had only been able to rest when he was sick.

One year, I remember, Allister was determined not to desert his family at Christmas, having failed them every preceding year, so he simply did not report for work on December 25. When he went to the mine on Boxing Day, the assistant manager was waiting for him.

"Here's your time and papers, MacDonnell," he said thrusting the documents into his hand.

"You mean I'm fired, Mr. Murchison?"

"Goddamned right. We don't want your kind."

"What about my family?" Allister asked. "I have nine children."

"'You should have thought of them yesterday," said Murchison, and turned into the office, slamming the door behind him.

Allister MacDonnell searched for three months for work, but found that the company had got there ahead of him and finally went into the woods to cut pulp, where he was killed by a falling tree.

His widow desperately tried to keep the family together on potatoes and molasses, but on the death of her youngest child from malnutrition, she sent two into a home, three others to her sister's, and went out to work scrubbing floors. When she died a year and a half later, only four of her children could be located to watch the plain pine box sink into the stony soil.

Maynard Scott's story was also testament to the impersonal monolith that was the coal company. He had worked in the collieries for thirty-six years when he died from silicosis.

Widowed the previous year, Maynard and his only son had struggled to keep the house and pay his son's medical bills. They seldom had heat, but when he died, his son, crippled with poliomylitus, was determined that the house should be warm for the wake. He hobbled down to the coal yard and begged for a small sack of coal to make the sparse front room hospitable for those who would come to pay their respects.

He was refused outright even when he had told the manager why he needed the coal, and when he offered to pay for it in weekly instalments of twenty-five cents, the manager laughed in his face and told him to be gone before the police were called.

In the end, I took up a bag of our coal and the young fellow fell at my feet crying with gratitude.

After we had the stove going and the guests were admitted, he stood erect, by the side of the casket, for twelve hours without sitting down or taking a break.

Coal took lives one way or another; directly by crushing men or gassing them, or indirectly through fatigue, arthritis, silicosis, heart failure, and in any combination of these. There is an old joke told in Boston and Toronto that you can tell a Cape Breton miner by the black around his eyes, but you can also tell by looking at his hands, for it is a safe bet that if his fingernails are not ringed with black then he has at least one finger missing.

Other men, of course, lost arms and legs, but at least half of all coal miners around here now suffer, or have suffered, from back trouble, and if I had a dollar for every vertebra that was damaged and every spinal fusion carried out, I would be rich.

Although we were aware of the everyday dangers which faced us, when working the pit we seldom gave thought to the possibility of being killed; that is to the possibility of yourself being killed. Just like the soldier or seaman, we said to ourselves, it couldn't happen to me.

However, when an accident did occur and the word was passed up the level that a man was dead, I would involuntarily twitch and take a quick glance at the roof. At a moment like that a man is truly alone because he realizes that if he was relieved because the victim was someone else, so would his buddy be relieved if he was killed. Only on the surface would I feel sorry for the victim and hate myself for my underground feelings.

Once, in my younger, wilder, irreverent days, I was caught in a fall and had my legs badly crushed. I was taken to St. Mary's Hospital and laid on a table affair while sisters and doctors rushed around me like ants round a jam pot.

When I came to consciousness an old nun was bending over me, a huge cross swinging from her neck and a ferocious frown stamped on her face.

"What religion are you?" she demanded. "Catholic, isn't it?"

"I have no religion, Sister," I replied for reasons which were not then, nor now, clear to me.

"For shame!" she cried hoarsely. "I know you, Donald Ross, and you're a good Catholic."

"All right," I sighed, "then why did you ask me if you already knew?"

"Don't talk back to me, young man," she snapped, "just tell me how long it is since you took confession?"

"Well..." I looked around for something to save me from the truth, but seeing nothing, finally admitted, "three years, six months, and two weeks."

"Heaven save us!" she exclaimed indignantly. "I'll fetch Father Ranald immediately and you will take confession!"

"The hell I will!" I shouted, mad at being ordered around.

"Is that your real wish?" she asked icily.

"Damn right," I said, cross as a bitch with pups.

With that, she turned on her heel and marched out.

Just when I thought I would get some peace, the door opened and in she came, accompanied by three of her fellow sisters. "We are going to kneel here and pray for you until you see the error of your ways," the old nun announced piously.

Well, they kept it up for hours, taking it in shifts. When I saw that the old sister was taking double shifts and that they were far more stubborn than I could ever be, I broke down and agreed.

It was the best confession I ever had, and I threw in some spicy bits to cheer the priest's day.

5: Cook dem like fish

There were four collieries in our town during the zenith of the industry; "A" colliery, "B" colliery, the Dump, and the Glory Hole, and the neighbourhood around each mine took on the name of its respective colliery. Between these small neighbourhoods, each with about six hundred people, existed a bitter and undying rivalry.

Ball games, held on the flattened Victoria Mine, were played with few suggestions of good will, little degree of sportsmanship, and with virtually no regard for the rules of the game. The referees had to be imported from one of the neighbouring towns for had they been local men they would certa nly have been killed for alleged favouritism.

Boots, fists, bottles, and lumps of clinker flew in all directions, and after a series of chronic injuries, the police wisely put a stop to the "games."

Outlaw the ball games they might, but the police could never stop the fights which almost approached gang warfare. A boy from the Glory Hole would not dare venture into another area without being accompanied by at least two of his buddies. At any of the numerous dances held over town, a cry of "Dump!"

would indicate a boy in trouble calling upon any of his own district to come to his aid. Violence invariably followed.

Sometimes the fights were terrible spectacles and once, through the night mist, I saw three "A" boys throw a prostrate young man over a wall. I couldn't identify them so I kept my mouth shut.

The Idle Times, as we termed the Depression years, was the period during which most fighting took place. Possibly it was due to men having no work to go to and getting bored with hanging about the rows and listening to their women complain.

It was also the period during which the people showed the most ingenuity, and when forced to find food from nowhere, it was surprising what we came up with. A quick foray into the country with light-ning raids on farms provided relief from idleness as well as from hunger. I would come home of a day and throw a dirty old gunny sack on the table and spill out seven or eight potatoes, a cabbage, a warm chicken, and an assortment of berries picked along the escape route.

We also bootlegged our own coal, selling it cheap to the merchants and anyone else who would take it. Needless to say, this was highly illegal as well as dan-gerous.

We would burrow into the cliff and drag the stuff out with only the most rudimentary timberwork to protect us from the temperamental roof. Sometimes we brought out a hundred bags a day from a sordid little gash in the cliffside and men would teeter up an almost sheer face, bowed down by the heavy, dirty sack on their shoulders.

One man fell backwards when he lost his balance, but, miraculously, Big Dan MacLean managed to stick out his hand and grab the man as he hurtled past.

One of our illicit workings was in the cliff upon which the convent stood, and after two or three months of labour we were so far in that the sisters said they could hear us scraping about below the kitchen floor. Terrified that the building was going to collapse, they fled to Father Andrew for assistance.

Grizzled and ancient, the old priest scrambled down the cliff and confronted us: either we stopped undermining the convent (and I guess he spoke both literally and figuratively because the nuns were close to panic-stricken) or he would take drastic action.

Father Andrew did not specify what this action might be, so we ignored him and continued mining.

Later that day, when we had lifted all our coal to the top of the cliff, we found out what he intended, for there he stood with three policemen.

We scattered in all directions and Father Andrew seized the coal and gave it away—as he told us later —to "the poor."

Little Frank MacKenzie commented to him that if that was the case he should have left the stuff alone because we were all poor.

Father Andrew muttered something about "unruliness" and scurried away, the stiff breeze flapping his soutane around his skinny legs.

One of the most fascinating things about a coal mining town like ours was its abundance of characters and, more amazing to the outsider, the widespread practice of giving almost everyone a nickname. While this practice taxed the inventive powers of the wits and wags and gave the place a colourful air, it also had practical considerations.

Its origin, of course, was in the Highlands, where men of the same name had to be distinguished from one another in some meaningful way. Now, as then, an Angus MacNeil would christen his eldest son Angus, and he in turn would name his eldest Angus. Their daughters might insist that their second sons be named after their father, so more of the same name would be born to confuse the issue.

A second son, Michael, would have less trouble unless his father was called Michael. Grandfather might then be known as Old Mickey and his grandson Young Mickey, or the boy might take on his father's first name as his second, in which case he would be Mickey Angus M. MacNeil.

If the boy married and his wife's name was Mary —or some other very common name—she might be identified as Mary Mickey Angus M.

To a large extent, however, time slowly changed these more traditional practices and men became known by some quirk in their nature, a physical defect, or some event in which they had been prominent.

In other cases, occupation or hobby accounted for the name; consequently, the Johnny Horse Shit Mac-

Donalds would all be descended from John who kept horses in his back yard. The Screwy Billies were likewise descended from a man who announced one day that the smoke from his chimney rose like a corkscrew.

After a while, the family or clan name would be dropped and men would be known only by the nickname. With the passage of still more time even men who knew others well, having worked with them all their lives, might not know their family names.

To compile a list of all the nicknames just from our area would take days, but off the top of my head I can think of dozens, both family and individual names: Ramcats, Pickle Arses, Saucy Jack, Lazy Sam, Satchel Arses, Big Pays, Dodger, Victory Queen, Red Jim, Black Dan, White Alex, Rannie John Js, Neilie Neils, Dut, Dit, Jit, Lewis Reels, Carbon Ears, Little Frank, Big Frank, Screwy Billies, Squits, Biffer, Boxer, Midger, Stood-the-Hots, Toots, Pooky, Packy, and so on.

In many cases the origin has been forgotten, in others deliberately buried. My father earned the name of Educated Tom, but despite the fact that it would be more applicable to me, it did not stick. My nickname was far less obscure than most; they called me Diamond Donnie—after a particular brand of rum.

Of all the characters, I found Newfoundlanders the most fun and the most generous. Some lived here permanently, but many more came to work in the mines just in the summer months. My work buddy,

Dan Joe Macintosh propounded the theory that they worked their summer, went home, stocked up with food and drink, and ate themselves to death during the winter. His evidence was remarkable and it was based on the fact that each year very few returned.

At the beginning of the "season" we decided to put this theory to the test and interviewed the Newfoundlanders as they arrived.

"Is Jack Snooks with you this trip?" Dan Joe would ask.

"No, my son."

"Where is he?"

"He'm did."

"Dead?"

"Arr."

"How about Israel Snow?"

"Did."

"And Lem Fudge?"

"Did."

"Are they all dead?" I asked incredulously.

"Don't rightly know, my son."

"See, I told you," said Dan Joe triumphantly.

"Well...I can't argue, but it doesn't sound right to me," I said sullenly.

"All dead," cried Dan Joe gleefully. "Every last one! Eaten themselves to death!"

Newfoundlanders gained themselves a reputation for being stupid, but for the most part this was grossly unfair. Even those who were had good reason: lack of education and opportunity, and almost total isolation during their upbringing.

One woman, Sally Fry, was a young widow of about thirty who lived alone in an unspeakable shack on the edge of the cliff. In those days I was less fastidious than I am today and I used to spend the occasional night there and so shared her welcome, warm ignorance with half the town. A fellow told me that one night he took some sausages for her to cook for his late snack only to discover that she had never seen a sausage before in her life. When she asked him how to cook them, not thinking he replied that she should fry them as she would fish.

When he sat down to eat she placed a plateful of frizzled skins in front of him.

"'What's this?" he asked.

"Sasges."

"But these are only skins. Where's the rest?"

"Yous told me to cook dem like fish, so I gutted dem."

Sure enough, he said, when he looked, there was a pile of skinless sausage meat lying on top of the garbage. He went to bed on an empty stomach but apparently it did not affect his performance, and Sally, blissfully ignorant, responded with generosity

Another time, Dan Joe and I were in charge of getting boxes to the Newfoundlanders who were loading coal like slaves. It was wartime and Dan Joe thought he would have some fun. When one of them came up, Dan Joe plastered a look of sheer horror on his face and made his hands tremble.

"What's up, me son?"

"'Terrible news," whispered Dan Joe in mock horror. "The Germans just captured Newfoundland."

"Well, well," said the Newfoundlander vacantly. "Dem Germans is divils, ain't dey? Is dere any more boxes here?"

Our coal industry has been studied to death and, in some cases, they even had studies to study the studies. We were studied by economists, by the church, sociologists, industrial consultants, by planners and psychologists, but mostly by government commissions. Nowadays, this great and beloved instrument of procrastination is widespread across the whole country, but I think we were the guinea pigs. We had the Rand Commission, the Gordon Commission, the Carroll Commission, the Duncan Commission, and the Donald Commission, and God knows how many more.

One as good as told us we all had to move away and live in Ontario, another that we had twenty years, yet another fifteen years, and so on until we were all sick and tired of hearing what was wrong with us and why we had to change. When it was too impolite to lay the blame where it really belonged, they exhorted us to paint our houses, cut our grass, and become moderate.

Well, we did and still industry and jobs did not come flowing in as we were led to believe they would.

Someone, some bright college type in Ottawa, decided that "attrition" was the answer and subtly, slowly, they chipped away and may keep chipping until there is nothing left. They put over a thousand men on "early retirement," then put hundreds more on a "compassionate pension," and as men died or retired, in half a century—before my very eyes, you could say—this land of mine, this strange, unique place of sadness which I still call my home, is being transformed from a loud, bustling, teeming hot-bed of activity and radicalism to a smouldering, whimpering spot on the map which, like an old, blind dog, is slowly rolling over onto its back, its heavy, tired paws one by one jerking in the air.

There's talk of a big revival for coal now. They've been going on about it ever since the Arabs got smart and hiked the price of oil, but I don't see very much action. There's a new mine coming, they say, but they've been after promising that one about a dozen times now. Maybe when I'm dead and buried you'll see it, but I won't, and I intend to hang around for a few years yet.

6: Bitter and bloody

When I was two years old there came to the shores of Cape Breton a man who was to have an impact upon our people the like of which I have not seen since. He was James Bryson MacLachlan, a giant among men, who inspired loyalty and dedication in others, who explained the intricate and the confusing to simple people, and who, while offering little but sweat, turmoil, and tears, held out to the miners and their families a hope of a better day, a new order, a vision of a society, just and happy and well-fed.

More than this, I think, Jim taught us that the working class had its own dignity; that a proud, upright workman, with straight back and head high, not only was well-worthy of his hire at good, honest rates, but was equal in the sight of whatever creator there might be to the pomp and pageantry of the top hats and fat bellies and gleaming watch-chains. Jim told us that we were not, as many of us had supposed, cattle to be beaten and herded as the property of the company, but free spirits whom natural and inviolable laws decreed had the right to resist being trodden upon, the right to demand return for our labour sufficient to feed, clothe, and shelter our families in decency, and the right to claim our say in the decisions which governed our lives.

Ironic it is, I guess, that Jim came to us in a cattle boat along with dozens of other emigrant labourers seeking an honest living in the New World. He docked at Sydney Mines and went to work in Princess Colliery, sending for his family when he had saved enough for the passage. After a while, he moved to Glace Bay and it was there I first met him.

I must have been about twelve at the time, although it is none too clear in my mind now, when I went with Daddy to see Jim at his home in the Bay. Daddy had some kind of problem with an overman and had gone to seek Jim's advice. I was not involved in the conversation, having been sat on a chair against the wall, but every now and then Jim gave me a sharp glance as if to say "Watch your step!"

Of course, he was fairly young himself at that time —must have been in his early forties—with a full head of hair and a back like a ramrod. It is hard for me to recall his appearance then exactly but I do recall he seemed very serious and forbidding.

What I also remember is that the room was filled with books. Books on science and politics, theology, astronomy, economics, Greek, mathematics, and church history. Jim, I found out as time went by, knew something about almost everything and there were damn few who, educated or not, could hold their own in an argument with him. I remember Reverend Mercer and Reverend Swain, both strong supporters of labour, being floored by Jim's knowledge of theology and of the scriptures.

It wasn't until the thirties that I got to know Jim well and I had dealings with him almost up until the time he died. I can see his face before me now, thin and gaunt, with small chin, protruding ears, and high, sloping forehead. He had a big bulbous nose, a full moustache which completely covered his upper lip and, under bushy, tangled eyebrows, two large, shining, hypnotic eyes. The eyes I will never forget: they could be red-rimmed, rheumy, and misty; flashing with rage and passion; or steady and accusing.

I have often remarked that Jim and Daddy had a great deal in common, although Daddy was a little taller and, of course, his accent was completely different.

Daddy used to love telling stories about Jim. He knew his history down to the last breath and needed no excuse to regale all and sundry with his knowledge. Jim MacLachlan is to Cape Breton what Norman Bethune is to Canada. Officially his existence is barely acknowledged, the well-to-do of my son's generation have never heard of him, nothing is taught about him in the schools, and the last time I looked, the Miners' Museum over in Glace Bay didn't even have a picture of him on the wall. But those who know about him revere him like the Indians revere Gandhi and those that revere him are well-versed in his life story. My father was close to being a worshipper.

I well remember one of the times Daddy gave me the Jim story. I came into the house one snappy February afternoon, huffing the cold off me and looking for a sit down and a warm. Tom and Alex MacKenzie were in the kitchen argybargying about "The Belle of New York," and whether or not Marion Davies was the most beautiful woman in the world.

Well, my views on the subject were well-known and I wasn't too welcome in that company. I never had much use for Marion—the boys called her by her first name as though she lived two doors up— even before she got mixed up with that Hearst fellow and a right maniac he was if ever there was such a thing.

Ma was in the parlour with old Mrs. Permberton from down the row. It was nice and warm in there, but blessed if I could sit there listening to old Mrs. P. rambling on about how her eyes had got better since she started using BonOpto tablets and how Ma should still be feeding us Syrup of Figs. My Lord, the stuff they used to go on about when they got a cup of tea in their hands!

Anyway, I shuffled on upstairs to have a lie down when I heard Daddy thumping about in the attic. He kept his books and magazines in cardboard boxes up there and every now and then would spend hours doing his "research." He'd been up there, on and off for a couple of days, looking up facts to refute some speeches Mackenzie King and Ernest LaPointe had made during a recent tour of the province, but by the sound of things he hadn't got what he was looking for.

I clambered up the rickety step-ladder and peered

in. "Jesus, Daddy, you're making quite the racket up here. Did you lose something?"

"Oh, it's you, b'y," he said, looking down at me, a strand of hair hanging over his nose. "I can't find a file I had on interprovincial trade."

"Interprovincial trade! By the jumpins that's heavy stuff," I said as I hauled myself through the hatch and up onto the planking.

"Maybe I gave it to someone at the local," he said, sitting down on a tea chest and mopping his forehead with a spotted kerchief. "Time for a blow anyway. It's warm work lugging this stuff around."

I plunked myself down on an old suitcase and took out my makings for a smoke. I was looking around for something to use as an ashtray when I saw a photograph of a cottage.

"What's that?" I asked, holding it out to him.

"That's a place called Ecclefechan, in Scotland. Your cousin Ivy brought it back for me a couple of years ago when she went on that trip with Dr. Douglas."

"Why she do that?"

"That's quite the house, that there," he said, a look coming into his eyes, "very famous indeed. That house, Donnie, was occupied by the great Thomas Carlyle. Heard of him?"

"Yeah, think so. A philosopher wasn't he?"

"Oh, he was a lot more than that, b'y. He wrote *The History of the French Revolution*. A brilliant work! Ah, the irony in that piece of writing. I've got it here some place; you should read it sometime."

"Maybe I will."

"But that's not why Ivy brought it back to me." He cocked his head to one side and gave me a knowing glance. "Do you know who was born in that house?"

"Yeah, you told me, Thomas Carlyle."

"No, no, b'y. He lived there right enough, but somebody else was born there. Guess who."

"Who?"

"Jim MacLachlan!" He was triumphant and flicked the photo back to me as if to suggest that a re-examination of it would show me that I should have known all along.

"Well, by Christ, so that's where he came from. When did he come here anyway, Daddy?"

"Nineteen hundred and two." Daddy reeled it off like a professor. "He was thirty-two when he cam to Cape Breton. From one coalfield to another. He was trapping in the pit at the age of ten, y'know."

"So were you."

"And a good many more like me, b'y. But Jim couldn't get work, see? That's why he came here. There was a bitter strike in nineteen hundred and one, all through Dumfries and Galloway. Of course, Jim was blacklisted."

"Just like here," I said.

"Just like here, b'y. Capitalism is the same all over the world," he said. Then added, "By definition, see? Any road, he got on a cattle boat and come over to Sydney Mines."

"Been here ever since."

"And been here ever since." Daddy took out his

pipe. "Got a bit o' time, b'y?"

"Sure."

And he was off, his hands drawing pictures in the air, regaling the dusty, cluttered attic with the MacLachlan saga. Much of it I already knew, some of it I had directly experienced, but when Daddy got going he was good listening. Besides, you couldn't get away from him even if you wanted.

Jim was involved in controversy and strife from the moment he arrived here to the moment he died in 1937. He was a man who had to be fighting for what he believed was right and it did not matter who or what was in the way. He fought union men just as hard as he fought the company men if he thought they were wrong and were selling out the interests of the rank and file, and he was a man who was never afraid to cast aside something he had once held close.

What he had personally built, he could tear down if it no longer served; what he passionately advocated one year he could denounce the next if he thought he had been wrong; men clasped to his bosom in one struggle could be spurned in the next if found wanting of the necessary principle and resolve.

He it was who slaved to build up the Provincial Workman's Association, especially on the Northside, yet he was the first to call for its destruction when he saw it had outlived its usefulness, its leaders had become corrupted, and its aims turned awry. Once convinced that this was so he threw himself into the fight to eradicate the P.W.A. from the face of Cape Breton and in 1906, he was corresponding with the United Mineworkers Union in Indianapolis, trying to get that organization to come to Nova Scotia.

Oh, the fights were bitter and bloody between the old guard led by John Moffat and the young turks led by Jim MacLachlan, with all manner of manoeuvring, argy-bargy, legal footwork, and even, on occasion, fisticuffs.

Daddy told me that there was one meeting of what they called the Grand Council of the P.W.A. in Halifax when he and Jim and a bunch of others from Cape Breton were refused recognition, and they spent four days arguing over the credentials. Finally, Daddy said, they were ordered out of the convention hall but, naturally, refused to leave, and when they went to the convention the next morning there were police there who refused them admission.

While Jim, Daddy, and the others were fuming outside, Moffat and the old guard had themselves all re-elected and passed resolutions declaring Jim and his followers to be illegal.

He finally succeeded in bringing in the United Mineworkers and, some three years or so after his ejection from the P.W.A. convention, Jim was elected secretary-treasurer of what later became District 26 of the U.M.W., a position he was to hold—on and off —for several decades. Within a few more years he had brought about a merger of the old P.W.A. and the U.M.W. to form the First Amalgamated Mineworkers Union, later still, established the U.M.W. once more and, bless my soul, even later, was trying to get rid of the U.M.W. and bring back the Amalgamated. He was always on the move, was Jim.

Excitement there was aplenty for MacLachlan's growing family, but there was also hardship. As early as 1909, he was blacklisted by the Dominion Coal Company and was never permitted to work in the coal industry again and that, as usual, also meant there was no work from anyone connected with the coal company or in any way dependent upon it. He bought a small farm up on Steele's Hill (his family are there yet) and for a while had a milk round and sold a few vegetables.

In 1923, Jim was sent to jail. I didn't need Daddy to tell me about that because I was in it up to my neck, although I wasn't as close to Jim as Daddy was.

The Sydney Steelworkers were on strike at the time, having been driven by the most barbarous treatment to walking off their jobs. The provincial government had expanded the provincial police force at the request of the Sydney Board of Trade and, with a view (so said the premier) to "eradicating Bolshevism", dispatched them to Cape Breton on sand-bagged flatcars mounted with machine-guns.

At the head of this crowd of waterfront soldiers was one Colonel Eric MacDonald who, on arrival, teamed up with Captain D.A. Noble to institute a reign of espionage and terror. Noble was a man whose name belied his nature and who lives in local legend as one of the most feared and hated wherever labour raises its standard.

Harassment and beatings were common and the most vulnerable were picked for firing. Roy (the Wolf) Wolvin, BESCO's president, intended to stand for no nonsense and announced to the press that trade unionism was wrong in principle and would not be tolerated.

June was hot that year and towards the end of the month things boiled to a head with battles breaking out all over the city: between strikers and scabs, between strikers and police and, pretty soon, with federal troops, too. The men took over some parts of the steel plant but were driven out by the provincial Goons, mounted on horseback and wielding clubs, chains, whips, and iron bars.

I was there and I saw it. I did not see what happened the following day, but Daddy did.

He and Jim MacLachlan had gone in to Sydney to meet with the steelworkers' leaders to see what help, if any, the miners could give them. Daddy said it was a quiet evening, with not much of anything going on except people returning home from church and others lounging around in their front yards.

Suddenly a large troop of mounted provincial police rounded the bend and charged at full gallop into the churchgoers, smashing them down with poles and clubs. Not satisfied with this, they tore down the fences in front of the little houses, smashed the windows, and even came into the houses to attack the occupants.

My aunt, who lived on the street, told me later that one Goon tried to ride his horse through the passage and into the front room, but only succeeded in destroying her door, fence, and hall stand. One very old woman was deliberately beaten into the very dust by three troopers, while a pregnant girl was thrashed with a long pole and gave premature birth to a child which died. A young boy of about ten was trampled under the hooves of the horses and left a bleeding pulp in the gutter.

MacLachlan returned to Glace Bay as fast as the rented trap would carry him and by breakfast of the next day he had organized mass meetings through-out the coalfields. The men were livid when they heard what had happened in Sydney and, as a result of the outcry, Jim and Danny Livingstone dispatched telegrams to every local in the District, calling the men out and urging them to fight the brutality of the government.

Within a week, not a single coal miner was at work in Nova Scotia.

As soon as he heard of this, Premier Armstrong ordered the arrest of Livingstone and MacLachlan for "unlawfully publishing false tales, which were likely to occasion public mischief."

Late that night, Danny and Jim were working at the District Office when a man came in and told them they were wanted outside in the hall. The second they poked their noses through the door they were seized, gagged, and bound, and carried down the rickety old stairs and bundled into waiting cars which tore through the night, a hundred miles over abominably rocky roads, to the Strait of Canso, where they were put on the train for Halifax.

Both bail and a writ of habeas corpus were denied the union lawyers and Jim and Danny were given neither bedding nor food for several days. About five days later, however, the lawyers did manage to get them out on bail—$4,000—and they came back to Cape Breton to wait for the trial.

My Lord, what a reception we gave them when the train landed in Sydney, with brass bands and flags, and what a great mass meeting we had that night in Red Square, behind the post office. Daddy was like a kid with a new toy, beaming from ear to ear, calling Jim "the greatest leader of the century," and ecstatic over the fact that the western Canadian miners had come out in sympathy.

Premier Armstrong's stupidity and MacDonald and Noble's barbarity had resulted in not only two thousand steelworkers being off the job but also every single coal miner in the Dominion of Canada.

It was just at that time when union solidarity started to mean something more than words that the beetle-browed John L. Lewis struck by revoking the District charter, placing our union under trusteeship, firing Jim and Danny Livingstone out of office, and ordering the men back to work. Never was there such a bitter pill to swallow.

To add insult to injury Lewis had asked Roy Wolvin to co-operate with him in cleaning up the District and, naturally the Wolf (who believed unions were wrong in principle) was only too happy to oblige by stopping the checkoff of dues and diverting the money to Lewis appointees.

Lewis dragged poor old Silby Barrett out of the pasture and made him provisional president, giving him full power to run an organization that hated his guts. The less said about Silby the better; I always found him a fine fellow to get along with, but he had more heart than brains and not an atom of class consciousness...no doubt he would have met the charge on Bloody Sunday with the Marquis of Queensberry's Rules.

By around July 20, it was all over. The pits had gone back to work one by one, by hook or crook, by threat and blackmail. The steelworkers were annihilated. The Sydney newspaper announced "Crisis precipitated by Red Assassins from Moscow," and the powers that be got ready to send Jim MacLachlan to the pen, out of harm's way.

It was mid-August before the initial hearing was held and, by then, the charges had been changed to seditious libel. It was not until October that the trial actually got under way after a delay caused by waiting for Colonel MacDonald to return from his vacation in Fort Lauderdale.

Neither Daddy nor I could get to Halifax for the trial, but Red Dan told us it was a kangaroo court from start to finish. The attorney general prosecuted and the judge was a former lawyer for the coal company. The attorney general, Wally O'Hearn, was among the most fanatical and twisted of red-baiting Liberal horse droppings and, apparently, built his case around the allegation that on one of the many raids of Jim's home by the police they had found some documents from the Third International and a red flag.

"There was no red flag," Jim said from where he was standing, guarded by police on either side. It was all he ever got to say throughout the entire trial and he was duly pronounced guilty as charged.

O'Hearn, Wolvin, and the Sydney *Post* demanded the maximum twenty years' imprisonment, but the judge was a little smarter—I guess he didn't want a civil war on his conscience—and gave him two years in Dorchester penitentiary.

The case was appealed but was rejected out of hand. It was not surprising: five of the seven judges had worked for the coal company. The case was then taken to the federal cabinet and MacLachlan was released. He had served three months of his sentence.

To say that the track was lined with people from New Brunswick to Glace Bay would only be a slight exaggeration, for the working people of this province turned out in their thousands to welcome Jim MacLachlan back into their midst, where he belonged.

The day he got back to the Bay not a miner reported for work and eight thousand people marched through the streets, led by six brass bands and Jim hoisted on the shoulders of his admirers. My God, I don't think I have ever seen such a throng in all my days!

Despite the fact it was a bleak and blustery March day, they poured out of the brown and green company houses with their kids and their dogs whining and scampering around their legs. It was like a civic holiday and though the forbidding clouds lowered over us, our communities wore a communal smile. Jim was home!

In the light of what I have already related, it would be rather senseless to suggest that Jim did not have a reddish tinge about him. The fact of the matter was that for many years he was a member of the Communist Party—as was my father, who used to ask how a man with any sense could be anything else in those times—and he often looked to Russia for inspiration. Once, I remember, in 1922, Jim sent a telegram to Lenin, asking the Russian government to underwrite a $15-million loan to help ease the widespread distress in Cape Breton at the time.

I guess Vladimir Illych was busy with his New Economic Plan or Stalin's intrigues at the time, for I don't believe Jim got any response.

I have often wondered how Katie MacLachlan fended for the brood during those tough times and also what kind of arguments she and Jim had over the years. Did she ever urge him to give it all up, to put his family first, to let somebody else fight the battles, lead the way? She was certainly much more supportive than Ma, who balked and checked Daddy every inch of the way, but there must have been times when even Katie thought Jim was a man possessed, blinded by the crusade, crazed with mission, obsessed by the horizon to the extent of ignoring what lay about his feet.

I do not know, nor, I think, will any of us ever know. Today, Jim's descendants are a fairly close bunch when it comes to family matters. They do not gossip, nor are they anxious to rake over old coals. They all have his dash of nobility about them and his stubbornness.

There is also, I think, a touch of bitterness and hurt. It is small wonder.

7: She's on, Donnie

Strike!

The word came rumbling round the rows like an old bumble bee on the wind, being passed from house to house over the back fences and through the washing lines, and being shouted out to the old men on the front steps by Roddie Willie, as he tore away down the middle of the snowy, muddy street.

It was 1925, and I was still nursing my wounds from the 1923 strike. Daddy and the older fellows were scarred yet from the struggles before that. I guess we were what they call "battle-hardened", but, by Jesus, we weren't ready for this one.

We were no strangers to the word strike—God knows, we had lived it, eaten it, and breathed it in the pit, at home, in the tavern, and on the ball-fields —but we didn't know the meaning of that word until 1925. It was the most memorable year of my life and I can recall it better than this last one that's gone.

There are more good reasons to forget it than you can shake a stick at, but just as well try to get Beano Taylor to go on the kag.

I can't remember what day of the week it was now, but the fifth day of March sticks in my mind. I was just turning in at the gate, paddling through the filthy slush in our little front yard, when I heard Roddie Willie screeching behind me.

"Strike! Strike!" he hollered, staggering at breakneck speed over the churned up wheel ruts.

"Stop for Jesus' sake, will you!" I yelled at him as he was going by me, and he swung around, doing a little dance in a puddle, eager to talk yet anxious to be away.

"She's on, Donnie, b'y. Hundred per cent!"

"Take your time now, Roddie," I said, getting a grip on his arm to stop him flying away down the row. "Where do you get this story from?"

"Downtown," he said. "I was hearing them talk on the corner. Mr. MacLeod hisself said the order has gone out. Starting tonight."

"And it's a hundred per cent, you say?"

"Sure is. I heard him and Alex MacKay and Joe Nearing telling a bunch of fellows that they're pulling everybody out. 'No pumps! No fans! they was saying."

I stood and watched him go, careening through the sludge, shouting at anyone who would listen. He slipped and fell headlong into the mire at the corner, but was up in no time and was off again, splashing and raving out of sight behind Jenkins' barn.

I don't know why it took me by surprise. I should have known it was coming two days earlier when I went into the New Aberdeen company store with Vic Matthews and saw the sign posted over the wicket: NO MORE CREDIT. It was enough to send a shiver down your spine because it meant starvation to the many who were behind in what they owed and to pretty near everybody if they went on strike.

The company had picked out three pits, Number Two, Caledonia, and Number Six, to suspend the credit the company store normally extended to the men in slow times; the others went on as usual—the company granting credit in slow or idle times and collecting it back when things picked up again. However, the men who worked in these three collieries were different: they were trouble-makers, militants, leaders, and it was clear they had to be punished.

Not only was the credit suspended at these three stores, but what made it worse was that these men owed more than their fellows at the other pits—pretty near $200,000, they said, by the late spring of 1925.

While the other pits had been working an average of twenty days a month, the men in Caledonia, Number Two and Number Six only worked about seven, and in February of that year, while the others worked eighteen days, these mines only got four days' work. The debts had been mounting up at the "pluckmes," and most of the men would go for months without ever drawing any actual pay.

Daddy and I were lucky because the Dump colliery had worked twenty-three days in January, and twenty-one in February, and all we owed between us was for a bit of powder to replace the bum lot I had got the week before. My brother worked in Number Two colliery and owed the company over fifty dollars, a debt it was to take him years to pay off.

When the notices went up, of course, Daddy and I had to carry brother Tom because with no money and no credit he was not able to contribute a thing to the household expenses. Ma, true to form, said it was no more than he deserved for mixing with a bunch of reds. I could hear Daddy grind his teeth on his pipe stem as she was prattling on, but, like me, he knew there was no point in fighting with her because she would never change.

The no-credit notices were posted in direct response to the union's rejection of the company's latest offer. The management of the British Empire Steel Corporation had "offered" a cut in wages of ten per cent. The union refused to even consider such a proposal—the men would have lynched them if they had. The negotiations, if you could call them that, had been going on since the previous November when the company's first proposal had been a wage cut of twenty per cent. Later they lowered this to fifteen per cent and finally to ten.

The Minister of Labour in Ottawa had appointed a board of pro-BESCO businessmen, but even they had to admit defeat and told the honourable gentleman that there was nothing they could do to avert the impending confrontation.

The men were desperate because, under the so-called "Montreal Agreement," which had been signed in 1921, a day's pay was set at $5, and yet four years later we were working for $3.70 a day and faced a further reduction to take us down to $3.33 a day before deductions. It was a life of utter misery for those families where there was only one pay coming in and the men were inno mood to give in.

When I went into the room Daddy was sitting in a corner, scraping his boots onto a piece of newspaper and noisily sucking away at his old black pipe. He looked up at me in that strange bird-like pose he had, his moustache quivering on his upper lip.

"Well? What's all the commotion?" he asked. "There's being enough shouting outside our house to last for a week."

"The strike's been called."

"Ah, that's it, is it?" He moved the pipe from one side of his mouth to the other. "Not surprising. I thought it'd be today or tomorrow."

"Jesus, Daddy, you'd think they'd wait a little bit and let us put a bit by us before we hit the streets," I said.

"Listen, b'y, you don't know what you're talking about," Daddy said sharply. "Are you living in a dream world or something? We're locked out."

"Yes, I know. Three pits."

"No, all over. Not only here but Waterford and Sydney Mines, too."

"I didn't know that."

"Too busy chasing girls, no doubt," he said severely. "There was another nine pits closed today and notices posted at the stores in Reserve and Passchendaele."

"What about here in the Dump? There was nothing said down the local."

"That we shall find out soon enough," Daddy said grimly. "Herself will be coming in at that door any minute. And before she comes, I guess this is as good a time as any to tell you you're remarkably ill-informed for someone who is an officer of the union."

"Well, I only stopped by the hall for a minute so I didn't get all the dope."

"Where have you been since the crack of dawn?"

"I was out to Morien."

"Seeing the MacIntosh girl again, eh?"

"Yes." I felt uncomfortable under his stare, but was determined to fight back. "But what's wrong with that? For God's sake, Daddy, I'm twenty-five years of age. You had kids at my age."

"I'm not saying you can't get married if you want, Donnie." He put the boots down and took the pipe out of his mouth. "All I say is this: number one, times are bad and not likely to get better, at least for a while; number two, I don't think she's the kind of woman you'll get along with—she's too much like your mother; number three, you've accepted serious responsibilities in your local union and 'tis nothing short of a disgrace that you spend so little time at it, especially now when trouble is brewing."

"I'll do my best," I said. "But you know how they always go to you first with anything even though I'm supposed to be the secretary. Jesus, I think we should switch."

"It's up to yourself," he said with a wave of the pipe, "but don't hang onto it if you're not going to treat it with respect."

"I'll keep the job until the strike is over."

"That might be for a long time, Donnie, this is going to be as bad as nineteen hundred and nine. She's going to be dirty and no mistake."

Daddy had told me about the 1909 strike before and, even though I was only a little fellow at the time, I can remember the bitterness that blackened the souls of the people around me. There was a twelve-hour day then, no contract, and a cost of living which went up four times the rate of the wages.

That strike was all the more bitter because there was a division within the ranks of the miners, many of the older men opting for the "no strike" pro-company policies of John Moffat's Provincial Workmen's Association while the younger fellows like Daddy followed Jim MacLachlan and the radicals in the United Mineworkers.

Needless to say, the company refused to recognize any but their old friend Moffat and there was a bloody tie-up with scabs, spies, saboteurs, and the army. The county had sworn in over five hundred special constables to help the company and the government in Ottawa sent in the militia to try to take over the towns. They had put up electrified fences around the collieries and kept the scabs in disgusting and unhealthy conditions in special compounds, and Daddy told me the Board of Health authorities demanded an end to them, they were considered so bad. There were riots, outbreaks of typhoid, machine-guns, marches, and one of the managers' houses was even blown up.

Months later the men crawled back, utterly beaten.

There had been two further strikes since then—which I can remember much more vividly—and the famous slowdown in 1922, when the Minister of Labour had accused us of employing "underhanded and dishonest means of sabotage." Jim MacLachlan had put him in his place by firing off a telegram saying, "A miner has a perfect right to work with his coat on if he wants to!"

The slowdown was also undertaken to protest a wage cut—on that occasion a reduction of over thirty per cent! It is hard to imagine such a thing taking place.

I hear some fellows saying that we have grown soft over the years, but I am sure that the miners today would tear the place to pieces rather than suffer a wage reduction of that magnitude. No wonder that even that old reactionary Arthur Meighen was prompted to tell the House of Commons that the slowdown was all right with him because he figured it was only fair for the miners to give two-thirds of a day's work for two-thirds of a day's pay. I don't imagine that was too well-received in the Tory business circles of Sydney and Halifax.

They were stirring times, all right, and I was fairly active in the local, attending the meetings, running errands, and listening to speech after speech. The Bolshies were very active during the slowdown and it seemed like whenever you turned around Jim and Red Dan were propagandizing.

They had been recruited, apparently, by "Moscow Jack" MacDonald, a fellow who came down from Toronto, whirled his way through a couple of dozen meeting halls, and swept off again to convert the rest of the world.

I remember Daddy and I were among the delegates from "A" colliery local to the District convention in Sydney. It was glorious summer weather and the tempers were as hot as the sun. What a donnybrook she was! There was more screaming and shouting at that meeting than you could shake a stick at. I have never heard the like before or since, and the abuse which was heaped upon the executive was not fit (although I admit I did my share of heaping).

Tim Buck was there as a fraternal delegate and held the floor for over an hour describing the wonders of the Soviet Union. It was pretty heady wine for a bunch of fellows who had just had their pay cut by a third, who could hardly put food on the table, and could see little hope in the months ahead.

My goodness! A land of plenty, awash with food, money, and happiness. Unemployment had been abolished and now, Comrade Buck told us, the workers, instead of taking orders from the boss, were now giving the orders; those who had previously sat in the office now wielded the pick, those who had kept the accounts now handled the shovel, and those who had previously been manual dirt under the overseer's boot were now deciding policy and managing the business.

I doubt that many of the men, even in their desperation, found all this totally convincing, but it was great stuff and the ranks were roused and cheered by it. Daddy nodded vigorously throughout and I could tell that, even if he didn't swallow it whole, he certainly wanted to believe it.

The convention got so carried away with visions of the new order that they voted to send Jim MacLachlan as a delegate to the next Red International of Trade Unions congress in Moscow, although I am not sure where they thought we would get the money from.

Anyway, the president, Bobby Baxter, issued instructions that there would be no strike, but the Number Two local ignored the edict and, over the heads of the executive, called the men to a mass meeting on the ballfield in Glace Bay. There must have been six or seven thousand of us there, and were we spoiling for a fight. It was almost unanimous: strike!

That night Daddy and I trudged across country to the sand bar where another four thousand men had gathered and, if anything, they were even more belligerent than we had been earlier in the day.

As of midnight, twelve thousand men were out across the province and, true to form, the next day in trotted the cavalry and up went the machine-gun nests. Within two weeks it was all over; the men had forced the wage cut down from thirty per cent to eighteen per cent.

Even though the men had ratified it, Red Dan condemned the settlement, saying its acceptance was due to the fact that it had been offered "under the muzzles of rifles, machineguns, and gleaming bayonets."

That had only been two years earlier and here we were at it again. It seemed that one bit of trouble ran into another and that the company would never be satisfied until we had all starved to death—although who would have mined their coal for them if we had, God only knew.

But did they want to mine coal? One theory had it that they couldn't even sell the coal they had banked and welcomed a period of idleness to cut costs and drive up the price. The story was that all over the world markets were dwindling and the price had plummeted.

The immediate cry had been for the protection of the shareholders, those anonymous but sacred individuals whose interests always came first even if it meant wage cuts and layoffs. The British Empire Steel and Coal Corporation, never slow to lead the fight for shareholders and the lowering of wages, reluctantly announced the cuts and, with usual references to "outside agitators," had cut off credit, locked the collieries, and sat back to wallow in the righteousness of their own cause.

The company's willingness to force the strike should have told us something, but we were so desperate that I guess most men figured it didn't matter whether they starved at work or starved on strike. We should also have been warned by the company's state of preparation for the strike, because as early as January they had polled their officials to see if they would scab and had pulled all the pit horses out of the collieries and stabled them at a farm just outside of Sydney.

All the signs indicated that BESCO welcomed the stoppage with open arms, and cautious men said we were walking straight into a trap, but it was clear most men were in no mood for caution and that they agreed with Jim MacLachlan who said they had only two choices: "crawl or fight."

Four days after the strike had been called the Wolf and BESCO general manager J.E. McClurg asked Premier Armstrong to send in troops and provincial police for the protection of what they called "outside men." While the company might not have been that enthusiastic about mining coal, it still needed scabs to maintain the pits in workable condition until such time as they might want to resume production. For once, the great class warrior Armstrong declined; he was planning a general election for late June and was playing all sides against the middle.

While Armstrong's rejection may have annoyed Wolvin and McClurg, it could not have bothered them too much, for BESCO had its own police force, and a more unsavoury bunch of cutthroats could scarcely be found. The Goons, as we knew them, were the very dregs and scum of society, drunks, thieves, smugglers, recruited from the Halifax waterfront where they were bribed and lured from their stinking, steamy, brawling hangouts around the infested wharves, stuffed into rough uniforms—lice and all—propped on horses they could hardly control, and shipped with rifles in their hands to wherever property was in need of protection.

At the head of this outrageous mob of legalized murderers was the detestable Captain D.A. Noble.

I was alerted to his presence by Napper Tandy, whom I met on my way to the union hall.

"Good day, b'y. Heard the news?"

"Good day, Napper. What news is that?"

"Noble be's here."

"Noble!" The contemptible name sprang from me with force equal to the gob of tobacco juice spat from Napper's lips. "When did he come?"

"Last night, they say. Snowy MacDougall says he was seen swaggering out of MacLean's bar, bragging as how he's going to clean up the strike and run the reds out of town."

"Times are bad, Napper, when the likes of that crawls into town." My gorge was rising at the thought of such a creature freely circulating in our communities and it steeled my resolve.

"'Times goin' to get a whole lot worse, too," said Napper, slowly nodding his grey head. "She's outright war now, b'y."

I left Napper cursing to an old dog by the steps of the church and wandered up over the tump and down into Devil's Kitchen.

As I was turning into the street where the union hall was I almost tripped over Saucy Joe MacNeil. He was grovelling about on his hands and knees at the edge of the road with the wind whirling the snow around him and making his hair dance.

"My Jesus, it's early to be hammered, Joe!" I said.

"I ain't hammered, Donnie," he said, almost crying. "I gone and lost a quarter and now I can't find the goddamn thing any place."

"Jesus, a quarter's going to be big money around here very shortly, b'y," I said, "and you throwing it about like a millionaire."

"Divine punishment, it is," he said. "I was just off for a few wet ones and suddenly it jumped out of me hand and rolled away."

"It's not likely you'll find it," said I, anxious to be away. "'The snow's the colour of the mud and so is the quarter by now. You'll be having to wait until spring before you get it again."

I knelt down and helped him look for a while, but it was no good; the more we stirred around, the dirtier everything got.

Saucy Joe straightened up with a hard, grieving sigh. "The trouble comes in gobs," he said, brushing off his pants, "what with the strike and all."

"No mistake," I said. "And it looks like Roy the Wolf has got us by the short hairs this time, Joe."

"That black bastard!" he spat in the gutter. "I knew as soon as that christer took over the company we'd never see any good times again. The bastard needs shooting and give me half a chance and I'd be just the laddybuck to do it, too!"

"Too bad somebody doesn't do it," I said. I gave him a slap on the back and carried on down the row towards the union hall.

Of course, I had never met Roy Wolvin, nor, I suppose, had any of the rank and file miners. I have never heard of him ever visiting one of the pits or touring the steel plant. He never seemed to take any part in civic activities or business club events and I did not know anyone who had ever laid eyes on the man, apart from the District officers who had met him in the course of negotiations. I once asked Silby Barrett what Wolvin was really like and he told me: "A clear snake, me son, a clear snake."

According to Daddy, Wolvin was thirty-nine years old when he took control of the industries that sustained the life of the people of Cape Breton and he came to us after a chequered career of wheeling and dealing and stock watering in central Canada.

I don't know why it should be so, but it seems to me that often the worst, most ruthless, most antilabour, are not those who inherited wealth and descended from an unfeeling and aloof aristocracy, but those who themselves sprang from fairly humble origins. Maybe it is because they were ashamed of their roots or had hated their childhood and wanted to wash it away by becoming stereotypes of the ruling class.

In any event, Roy the Wolf was such a man. He came from no great line of high financiers, nor from a rich family of any kind. He had no college education and by the time he was sixteen was slaving away as an office boy in a shipping company.

"You've got to hand it to the evil bastard," Daddy had said one day when we were going through the

Wolf's file in the attic. "He's no fool and that's for sure. Look at this. He took no more than about five years to get from errand boy to top dog in a dozen or more companies. It's all here, b'y, shipping, coal, iron, lumber, the works."

"Must have been pretty sharp, eh, Daddy?"

"Sharp is right, b'y, and crooked too, by Jesus."

"Why do you need to keep going through this stuff, anyway? I'm not sure as I need to know the black bastard's life story."

"You heard of the Talmud?" I shook my head. "Well, it's a religious book, see, like the Bible. It says: 'Know thyself.' You know what I say?"

"What's that?"

"Know thy *enemy*!" He waggled his finger, then tapped the file. "I got all this stuff from comrades in Toronto and I always keep it by me. Look at this. He's vice-president of this and chairman of that and secretary of the other and then, suddenly, at the age of thirty, what does he do?"

"Go ahead," said I, knowing there was no stopping him anyway.

"Ups and quits. Just like that, Donnie. The whole works. He resigns all positions and starts his own shipping company, and in three years—that's all, just three years—he controls the entire Great Lakes industry. Liquefying his assets, he was."

"Liquefying his what?"

"It's what I call watering the stock," he said with a gleam.

"Now I'm really lost."

"Watering the stock, b'y. It's what the big capitalists do when they want to shaft the little capitalists.
See, it's like this: he merges all the different companies into one—Canada Steamship Lines, he calls it—
but he declares the new company capitalized at
thirty-three million dollars. That's what he says it's
worth, in other words."

"So?"

"Well, b'y, see, the original companies were only
worth seventeen million. That means he squeezed
out of the shareholders sixteen million for him to
play around with. Did the same thing on the west
coast; smashed his way in there, then took over the
yards in Halifax, then moved in here. Oh, he was no
slouch, that laddybuck. It's all here. Take the file."

The war had been good to Roy Wolvin. While millions were being slaughtered in the trenches of
France and Flanders and the civilian population at
home was tightening its collective belt, Wolvin's
riches grew as he handled the shipping contracts for
the notorious Imperial Munitions Board. With his
war profits Wolvin bought up more companies,
gradually extending his influence, until six years
prior to the strike he joined the board of the Dominion Steel and Coal Company.

He had barely warmed his chair at the directors'
table when, with the help of Lord Beaverbrook and
some other English notables, he turned around and
bought the fifty thousand shares necessary to give
him control. Immediately he announced grand visions of a world-wide enterprise to be named the

British Empire Steel Corporation.

The Canadian Government rejected his application to charter this new company, but the Liberal administration of Nova Scotia was less resistant to his power and inducements. Charter in hand, Wolvin embarked upon a binge of company takeovers, once again watering the stock in the resulting mergers, until he had control over all coal, iron, steel and railway undertakings in the province. By the time the 1925 strike was called Roy Wolvin was feudal lord of Cape Breton and was the most powerful man in Nova Scotia.

Even though I had never met the man—had never even seen the man—I knew him, and hated him. His picture stared at me from the pages of the local papers: blacksuited with starched wing-tip collar, clenched jaw and cruel mouth, and those boring, beady, coal-black eyes that seemed to follow you around the room long after you had finished the paper and burned it.

With these thoughts swirling in my mind, I reached the end of the row and turned into the union hall. Tilted to one side in a very dangerous fashion, her steps were rickety and her shingles peeling. The building was in bad shape considering that it had not been there that long. I doubt if it was as old as me and I often wondered whether it had just been poorly constructed or if its deterioration had been caused by all the shouting and bawling which went on inside.

I found the union officers huddled around the

table, poring over the latest edition of the Sydney *Post*. None of them took any notice of me so I went up to the table and nosed my way through the bodies.

"What is it?" I asked the nearest head.

"McClurg's made a statement," said Charlie Anderson, glancing over his shoulder.

"A dandy!" Little Joe Poirier said ruefully.

"Good or bad?" I asked.

"Good or bad?" mocked Lem Murray. "Listen to him!"

"'Did you ever know that black son of a whore ever to say anything good?" Old Adam Francis whispered in my ear from behind.

"Oh, good day, Adam," I muttered, turning around to face him. "What's it all about?"

"I got the *Record* here," he said. "The statement's the same. Come by the side here and I'll read it to you."

"Go ahead."

"Now I don't know as how anybody actually heard the man say it," Adam began with his customary caution, "but here's what they say: 'Let them stay out two months or six months, it matters not; eventually they will come crawling to us. They can't stand the gaff!'"

A shiver ran down my spine and suddenly the hall felt colder. Whether he knew it or not, this company official, with his scowling eyes and ferocious moustache, had given us one of the most famous expressions ever known in these parts. "Stand the gaff" was to become a household phrase in Cape Breton for generations to come; a challenge to the stubborn spirit of our people.

"What do you think of that, b'y?" Adam looked at me, his eyebrow raised, his lips pursed.

"Jesus! She sounds bad," I said, grabbing the paper to get a closer look.

"She's bad, all right, Donnie," he said, fire coming to his eyes, and, losing his temper, he brought his huge fist crashing down on the table, scaring the others half out of their wits. "I'd kill him! I'd strangle the bastard with my bare hands if I could lay hold on him."

"Well, you won't, Brother Francis," said Ron MacKenzie, the local president. "He's much too well-protected for the likes of you to get near him."

"And with the taxpayers' money, too," said Joe Poirier."

"Yeah, that whore of a warden is swearing in specials again, I hear," Bo MacAulay put in.

"There's never been any doubt as to where that swine LeVatte ever stood," Ron said, shaking his head. "Pretty near the whole county council is bought and paid for by the company."

The Cape Breton county council, unlike the town councils of Glace Bay and New Waterford, had always been extremely pliant and had never wasted any time in leaping to the coal company's assistance. This odious body had been presided over for years by H.C. LeVatte, a man as anti-labour as Roy Wolvin himself, who, at the drop of a hat, would swear in special constables by the hundreds in order to protect BESCO's interests.

Waterford had men like Paddy Muise in elected positions and Glace Bay was fortunate enough to have majors like John Douglas or Dan Willie Morrison who were either labour themselves or sympathetic to the men. Since we were just outside the town's boundaries, we who lived in the Dump came under the authority of the County of Cape Breton and LeVatte's tender ministrations.

I took the paper to the back of the hall where I sat down and had a read of it. It seemed McClurg had been interviewed by some reporter who had compared the strike with a game of poker. "Game of poker, nothing," McClurg was reported as having responded. "We hold all the cards. Things are going to get better every day they stay out."

Then came the reference to our not being able to "stand the gaff." Asked what he meant by the term, McClurg explained that it meant the attendant hunger and privation. There was another statement in the paper by one of the other company officials who said the grass would grow through the streets of Sydney before the company would back down.

Fighting words, I thought, which added to my fears that the company did not want to mine coal and was more than happy to have an excuse to do nothing.

The District president John Willie MacLeod had issued a counter statement on behalf of the union: a defiant "No wage cut," and the newspaper had dressed it up and rewritten it to make it sound like the words of a raving bolshevik lunatic. The company held the whip hand and I knew in my bones there was no way we could win this one.

Standing the gaff was a rough business, as hunger became a way of life and dying children a matter of cold fact. The cries of the orators on the ballfields became ringing indictments of the capitalist system and a few called for arms to overthrow it. The local unions set up relief stations with what little they could procure and the wives lined up for their meagre share of the bare means of sustaining life: a bit of flour, a turnip, two potatoes.

Another household expression was born: "carrying the bag." They carried the bag for four months and there was damn little in it at the best of times, although God knows we tried hard enough to find stuff. Some of us formed foraging parties into the country to beg, borrow, and, quite frankly, to steal whatever food could be found.

I remember one morning in 1925, I was heading through Devil's Kitchen when I saw Danny Tracey come dancing towards me, whooping and hollering for all he was worth. It had been a particularly tough week and my bones were sticking through my skin so I was in no mood for his foolishness.

"Hold your coal, you silly bastard!" I shouted at him. "Do you suppose that's any way to be carrying on when folks are starving and babies are dying?"

"Good news, Donnie!" he yelled. "It's bread and bannock tonight, b'y."

"What in God's name are you talking about, man?" I was really getting riled. I never liked Danny at the best of times.

"Come up the tump and look into the siding," he said, grabbing my arm.

I followed him to the top of the rise and looked down. There, looking like big, black beetles, were five railway cars backed into the siding, each of them disgorging huge, white sacks into the arms of union officials and priests, who were stacking them on the back of a wagon.

I could scarcely believe my eyes. "What in the name of time is it?"

"Flour," Danny shouted. "Flour and oats. We'll be eating again, b'y!"

"Good God Almighty!" It was all I could say and I hurried on down the tump as fast as my feet would carry me, almost knocking Ron MacKenzie arse over head as I cannoned into the little yard. "Is it true?"

"See for yourself, Donnie," said Ron, opening the top of one of the sacks and lifting up a handful of flour. "It's a miracle, b'y!"

""Where in the Jesus did it come from?"

"Peterborough, Ontario."

"Who sent it?"

"'You're not going to believe this," said Ron, putting his hand on my shoulder.

"Try me," I said. "I don't care if the Devil sent it. God knows it's welcome here and may keep some little folk alive until the end of this mess."

"'The Quaker Oats Company."

"What?"

"'S'right, the Quaker Oats Company sent it down here because they heard things was rough. And it's free!"

"Well, long live capitalism!"

"Makes you think, don't it," he said with a shake of his head. "Maybe they're not all like the bastards we got to deal with here. But look lively, Donnie, get your coat off, and get this stuff loaded on the wagon. The sooner we can get it to the hall the sooner the women can be baking."

There were not too many pleasant events like that one, although unions across the country sent what money and supplies they could muster and the bishop had issued a pastoral letter calling for help.

The Wolf was wild and laced into Bishop Morrison, the Sally Ann, the I.O.D.E., the Hadassah, and all other organizations which he said had "taken sides" by extending any form of assistance. He found a ready disciple in the hateful LeVatte who told the Anglican synod in Halifax the hunger we were suffering was "divine punishment" brought about by an act of God because of the indifference of the people to the teachings of the church.

It was fortunate for the warden that ten of his special constables were guarding his own house, for some of the men would doubtless have crucified him to show him how well they knew their Bibles. I thought then, and think to this day, it was a disgrace the Anglican synod did not throw him bodily into the gutter for his blasphemy; and I think it even more remarkable that, after all this creature said and did, he died in his bed of natural causes. It speaks highly of the gentle and forgiving nature of Cape Bretoners.

Warden LeVatte and his county council were not alone in joining the efforts to starve us out, for neither federal nor provincial governments so much as voted a cent of relief to ease the burden, despite repeated appeals from the union and members of Parliament. Halifax blamed Ottawa and Ottawa blamed Halifax and as they did so more died. It was well that sympathizers across Canada and even in other countries were more generous or we would have perished in much greater numbers.

One contribution from an outside source was especially welcome to the lefties like my father and even gave those of us less romantically inclined a fleeting vision of a brave new world.

Daddy and I were sitting at the back of the hall because we were late arriving for the meeting. Ron MacKenzie introduced the District president who outlined the progress of the strike to date and repeated the District's determination not to concede one penny off the pay. He was given a good hand by the men who parted to let him out to go to another meeting.

Then Ron called upon Alex MacKay, the District secretary-treasurer, to address a few words to the local.

"Brother chairman," he said, in his loud buckish voice, "the financial situation remains very grim indeed. We are simply not after getting enough money coming in to buy the provisions necessary to keep body and soul together."

There was loud muttering throughout the hall, and several men shouted, "What about the International?" and, "Let Lewis pay."

"'I must remind the brothers here that the International Union is paying us forty thousand dollars a month," said MacKay. "And while I agree it's not enough, we must be fair about it.'

"Fair nothing!" shouted Oscar Lamey. "'That's not even a dollar each man a week!''

"And they paid nothing for the first six weeks!" my father said, his deep voice rumbling through the crowd.

"We are currently in the course of borrowing a hundred thousand," said Alex MacKay. "This was authorized by the District convention, and we should have it soon. But I must warn you this will have to be repaid after the strike by a general levy."

"We know all that, Brother MacKay," said Big Tommy Currie. "What we want to know is where the hell we're going to get more money to feed our families. Yous sent John Alex and that American across the country to go begging for us, but the crunch is that goddamn Welsh bastard Lewis won't pay us what is rightfully ours!"

There were cries of agreement all round the hall, with shouts of "Disaffiliate!" and "Down with Lewis!"

"Every man thinks of himself first," said Alex MacKay, "and that's only natural. But, Brother chairman, we must remember that there are two hundred thousand U.M.W. members on strike in the United States right now. Also, the International is fighting a very expensive legal battle against the rebel slate in West Virginia. The fact has to be faced, money does not grow on trees."

The growling grew louder and more violent and Alex turned to Ron and threw up his hands.

Just when it looked as if something ugly was about to happen I noticed the door open and Joe Nearing come in, red-faced and bustling with importance. He fought his way through the masses and finally got to the platform. I noticed he and Alex got their heads together and as Joe was telling him something, his face began to light up. He jumped up and held up his hands for silence.

"Brothers! Brothers!" The growling gradually subsided. "'I have an important announcement to make. I have good news which Brother Nearing has just brought me. It is that we have just received a most generous donation of five thousand dollars to the strike fund."

There was a loud cheer and stomping of feet. The mood was changing rapidly.

"Brothers, this is very touching, indeed," said Alex. "This donation has been received from fellow coal miners in another country." The cheering grew louder and Daddy gripped my arm. I glanced at him and he was nodding, a thin smile on his face. I looked around; others were smiling too. This $5,000 meant more to them than $40,000 from John L. Lewis.

"Brothers, this donation to you and your families

comes from the coal miners of the Union of Soviet Socialist Republics!"

The hall went wild. Men clambered onto the chairs. Hats went flying into the air. Adam Francis was thumping his stick against the wall. Daddy looked at me and there were tears in his misty blue eyes. He could see the millennium.

"Worker solidarity, b'y," he said, his voice quavering. "Hands across the seas. It will come in our time, Donnie."

Well, it did not come in our time, nor, I suspect, in any other will it come, but I am glad my father died still believing in that elusive thread of gold linking mens' minds and binding their hearts in the holy war for peace and plenty. The newspapers all said the money eventually was refused, but I am inclined to doubt it myself; the cash was too desperately needed.

The previous month the flu epidemic had struck and what had been tough conditions became appalling. The death rate had climbed rapidly and I had personally fetched the doctor to at least a dozen of our neighbours. Each time I came out of one of those company houses, the doctor by my side, my heart tightened another fraction, and the edge of my bitterness was sharpened. I used to study Dr. MacLellan's face, trying to detect any inkling of what was going on in his head, but he remained neutral to the end and if the pain and suffering of the children, the heartache of the mothers, the stench of death, and the anthem of poverty moved him, his face never showed it.

Of course, he too had been brought in by the company and was dependent upon them; his wages came from the checkoff on ours and his money was passed along to him by the company. Who was paying him now, during the strike, I knew not.

I surprised myself that I got along with old Doc MacLellan as well as I did for I am usually death on anyone who sits on the fence in time of crisis but we formed an interesting team; the young radical and the old, leather-faced, carpet-bagged medic.

The closest I ever got to him was the time Cissie Simms lost her little girl and I had taken him down the row, through the muck of the back yard and into the darkened kitchen, smelling of nothing but the cold. There was not a bite to eat anywhere in sight and the kids were dressed in flour bags. Cissie had lost her Jim the previous November in one of those growling black cave-ins in "B" Colliery and now she was losing her youngest, a bright little thing named, as the fashion was then, Euphemia.

Cissie wore a frock that was more patch than original garment, and the cloth was so threadbare you could see right through to her shrunken dugs and poking ribs. She was almost blue with cold and she looked like a chicken after all the meat had been boiled off the bones.

Old Doc fussed over the little one for a while, then drew back from the pallet shaking his head. He removed his spectacles and ran a hand across his brow..

"There's no use to telling you any lies, Mrs. Simms," he said gravely. "I am afraid she'll not be with us come morning."

"It's no more than I feared, Doctor," Cissie moaned, clutching herself with her bony arms. "Is there nothing can be done? Nothing at all?"

"No, my good woman," said Doc, fishing out his stopwatch and examining it. "It is too late. What might have been done is, of course, another matter."

"Might have? What do you mean, Doctor MacLellan? Is there something I could have done myself to stop this from happening? For God's sake, man, speak!"

"No, no," he gently put his hand on her shoulder, "there's no blame attaching to you, Mrs. Simms. It is just that if the child had been well-nourished she would have survived. Nobody is to blame that nourishment is not as plentiful as we would like."

"'Like hell!" I snapped. "Those murdering thieves at the general office are to blame. Don't be telling the woman nobody is responsible. Roy Wolvin killed your child, Cissie, killed her as sure as if he had come in here with a knife!"

"Donald!" Doc raised his great white eyebrows and glanced up at me. "This woman is in enough difficulty right now. She does not need a political lecture. Hold your coal and go to!"

I waited for him in the yard and when he came out I apologized for my conduct. He pursed his lips and ever so slightly shook his head as if to tell me he thought I was guilty of no sin. He clambered up into the trap and looked down at me, his old brown leathery face solid and inscrutable.

"That woman has had a hard time."

"That she has, Doc."

"Tonight she will lose that child and tomorrow night she will mourn it."

I nodded. It was unlike Doc MacLellan to dwell upon a case this way.

"The night after that she will be very lonely."

"Indeed," said I.

"Desperately lonely, Donald."

"Doc, what are you trying to say?"

"If you are not busy three nights hence, you might be good enough to offer her a little comfort."

I knew Cissie Simms for another fifteen years after that and there was not a person in Cape Breton upon whom I could rely more completely whenever I was in need. Dr. MacLellan, Cissie, and all her kin are dead now.

As time went on the newspapers became filled to bursting point with pious editorials, twisted news reports, and parcels of lies. Not only were we Bolsheviks, but atheists and bigamists, too. Not a day went by but that the press accused the strikers of some fresh outrage—as often as not invented by the editors. Buildings which were supposed to have been burned to the ground still stood when we went to check, men who were supposed to have been maimed and disabled still walked the streets, threats against the lives and families of company officials were written in one room of the newspaper's offices and typeset in another.

Slowly public opinion edged away from us and, fanned by most of the clergy and the Board of Trade, gradually became entrenched on the side of BESCO and law and order. From the few news reports we saw in other papers across Canada the impression was created that in the Cape Breton coalfields lurked a dastardly, hideous mob of fanatical and violent revolutionaries who, burning, raping, and looting at will, were planning a march of terror upon the capital to hoist the red flag and declare the Soviet.

It was far from the truth—although God knows why it should have been, there was ample justification for it—as most of the revolutionary talk was just talk, and, come summer, most of us were played out and ready to give up the ghost.

Not quite, though, for there were a few sparks of life in the corpse yet.

In those days there must have been close to fifteen thousand men working in the collieries of this island, shipping millions of tons to all parts of the world. Fifteen thousand strong-backed miners, who really could have marched on Ottawa and shaken things up had they only realized what power they possessed.

Today, there are only three mines and less than three thousand men. Fairly soon one of these collieries might close and the others could close themselves and then there would be no more coal; the pits would be levelled and the alders would scramble across the ruins like dirty green parasites gloating with their own virility and sneering at the misfortunes of man.

But we live in hope; we always did.

They told us our coal was too expensive, they told us it was too cheap; too much sulphur, not enough phosphorous; no good for steel-making, no good for thermal power; excellent for coke, but no coke markets; too far from central markets, too costly to bring up from under the sea; too hard, too soft.

It is a marvel to me if, as they said, our coal was so bad, that the mines kept going for over a hundred years and made millions of dollars' profit. In war-time, our coal was treated like solid gold, yet as soon as peace came it suddenly became second rate again.

Insult was added to injury when tons and tons of American coal were shipped in to feed the steel mill while mines were flattened and the payroll dwindled. In the Smokey River I saw stuff come out of the ground which we in Cape Breton would not have burned to melt the ice on the yard, or use on our driveways, yet the Japanese apparently could not get enough of it.

I have looked at the maps, talked to chemists, read shareholders' reports, studied the newspapers, and listened to the economists, but to this day I cannot make the slightest sense of it. If the production costs were small, if our coal was close to the shore and the surface, I am positive it would be considered perfect.

But, as Daddy used to say, that is the way it is when directors in London and Chicago decide they have skimmed the cream and find the milk remaining not worth the trouble. At the hands of men who had never even seen the places which produced their wealth, entire communities were sentenced to death with the stroke of a pen.

When I sit on the Dump beach and look over the water, it is hard to imagine that men, including my son, Will, are hard at work three miles out, the waves chopping far above their heads and the black dust in their eyes and noses.

In the deeper collieries, you don't get the sense of water above you, but in some of them, like the Dump pit, it was hard to dismiss the millions of pounding, thundering tons of ocean constantly trying to come down and crush you to death. Often I worked in two feet of water and frequently had to wade chest-deep through the dank, cold stuff, but that was not nearly as bad as having to work on your knees in it.

If a man dwelt on the thought of billions of pounds of pressure above his head it would probably drive him crazy, but most men put it out of their minds within the first month of work and never think of it again.

There was a time, when I was barrel-chested, cocky as spring, and as loud as Saturday night, when I thought I did have the answers. Seldom could anybody in the local put me on the spot and I could holler until the rowdiest mob was blasted into sullen silence.

Long John MacLeod was louder, but not as effective, for once off on a tirade he forgot what he was talking about. I would be in the chair, old wooden gavel in hand, and watch the veins on his neck stand out like roots of an old oak tree. The windows would rattle in their tired old frames and men would burst into laughter as Long John reached his incomprehensible climax.

As a private joke between Francie MacDonald and myself, I would always turn to him after one of Long John's speeches and ask loudly, "Did the secretary record all those vital points?"

Francie would nod solemnly, but when the minutes were read at the following meeting, the entry would be, "Brother MacLeod spoke at some length on matters of timely interest."

8: That mellow land

Although I drank with the best of them, partied as if there was no tomorrow, and tarried with many a woman in the haunts and hangouts of our town, it is not this place where I was born and where I have spent eighty years that gives me the fondest memories. For those, I think of the countryside, the unspoiled beauty of this island where neither coal nor tourist has yet taken a fatal toll.

Even today, with hotdog stands and chip wagons, motels and ski-slopes and auto licence plates from every province and state imaginable, those places of my boyhood and youth, where the sun shone in the wild fields of hay and the breezes rattled the windowpanes, are still good for a man to visit.

My grandfather's farm on the shores of the Bras d'Or lakes and my uncle's farm on the windy, rugged coastline of Inverness, are almost as they were when I visited them as a boy. To be true, they are both owned by Americans now who see their properties for a scant two months of the year, but their charms are virtually unchanged. Indeed, in a way, they are better now because the small spruce have encroached on once rich pastureland, and the barns and yards are overgrown with weeds and high grass.

To some this reversion to nature is unpleasing, for such people like the tameness of cultivation and need constant visual assurance of man's supremacy over his environment. But not me. I love the wild thistle and clover, the young green trees steadily marching back towards the cliff to reclaim their age-old territory, and the once bustling outbuildings now senile and weather-washed grey, slowly lilting into the waving, matted grass, and enjoying a quiet rest.

I have a quiet passion for old, worn out farms with their faded, peeling paint, rickety and fallen fences, overgrown yet cool, sweet-smelling wells, rutted roads, and leaning barns. Maybe it is because they are like me, almost at the end of their lives, long past their usefulness, and somehow reluctant to make any unnecessary changes.

I have no intention of buying a new sharply-cut suit, or wearing pointed shoes, or sporting a turtle-neck sweater down to supper. My old striped shirt without the collar is good enough for me now, and why should I be any different? If I was seeking something, applying for work or courting a young girl, I could understand taking the trouble, but all that nonsense is gone.

So it is with the old farms: why should they be painted spanking bright and get their old fields mown, their fences fixed and their barns repaired? Let them be, I say.

Oh, what it was to wake up early in the morning, rub the sleep out of my eyes, pull back the strange-smelling curtain and look out at a world, not of smoking chimneys and tall black pitheads, but of fresh fields of dew stretching away to the sea and the sun, bright and clear, calling every cow and bird to life. Scamper down to the old kitchen where my aunt would be frying bacon on the sparkling range, eat like a wolf at the huge, bare wooden table, and out into the yard.

I would stand, the wind making a mess of my town hair, and gaze away at the distant, glistening water, and, seeing a small fishing boat plying its way through the choppy sea, wish that I was out there, slippery, fresh, struggling fish jumping and dancing in my net.

Turning slowly around, past the good, strong barn with the black and white cows lining up for milking, I would stare up at the rolling green hills dwarfing the farm in their shadow. As the sun climbed rapidly it would pick out a clump of taller trees, lighting them a brighter green than their fellows, and quite quickly the whole side of the range of hills would be bathed in summer. If there were clouds they were usually clean and white, and as they rolled across the hilltops they streaked the richly wooded slopes alternately light and dark until the entire view became a kaleidoscope of changing shapes and colours.

Then I would set out down the dirt road towards the main track, kicking pebbles out of my way, and deliberately stomping in the tiny puddles which had formed in the ruts. When I reached the road—it was not paved in those days, of course—I would head directly into a thicket of tangled spruce, alder, and swamp. There were no paths through that patch of woods, despite my repeated travels, and I barged in a straight line through uncharted (as I liked to think) territory. Pausing for breath in the middle of a reedy bog, or caught in the dead and prickly branches of a whitened tree, I would cock an ear and listen. I needed no compass, for above the quiet sounds of the flies buzzing and the frogs croaking, came the muffled roar of the sea.

As the roar grew louder, I would come to a patch of rocky ground, clear of trees, and sporting only coarse grass. It was a clearing entirely surrounded by woods and marshes and visible only from the air. In my later years I speculated on what activities could be conducted here with complete abandon yet total privacy.

Then there would be a few hundred yards of woods and I would break out of the thicket, expectant and free, onto the cliff. The soft, springy moss, heather and blueberries, would bounce happily under my feet as I bounded down to the edge of the precarious cliff and, throwing myself down onto the green carpet, I would shuffle forward and peer over.

Sixty feet below, the frothing, swirling ocean would be pounding and thundering against the huge smooth-washed brown rocks, which perched one on top of the other, teetering and waiting to be sent crashing into the sea. The noise deafening in my ears, I would look out across the huge, twinkling expanse of deep blue-green beginnings of the mighty

Gulf of St. Lawrence.

I would pluck a tuft of growth from the very edge of the cliff and send it spiralling away, bouncing off the soft brown slopes, and eventually scattering itself into nothingness.

With the sea birds screaming and wheeling high over my head and the wind beating me dizzy, I would gambol along the cliffs all day long, dropping into sheltered hollows, crawling under stunted bushes and, taking my life into my hands far more than ever I did in the pit, painfully edging down the steep sides onto the tiny rocky beaches. There to sit, my coat flapping around me, with nothing to do but gaze in wonder, and dream childish dreams of lost continents, wild whalers, pitching and tossing on the deep, pirates, destroyers, submarines, and the endless sea reaching forever away to lands unknown, where palm trees swished in the breeze and men lived on coconuts and fish.

Just when the sun was showing its first signs of weakening, I would sadly, reluctantly, turn away from the ocean and slowly make my way back to the farmhouse. Coming up the old track, dragging a stick behind me, I could smell my aunt's cooking on the late afternoon breeze, and if anything in this world was designed to make a boy quicken his pace it was that smell.

My uncle would be finishing up around the yard and poke his face around the barn door, grinning broadly.

"Hurry along, Donnie, supper's ready!"

"Hurry yourself," I would call out, "better get that muck off your boots."

As much like a child as myself, he would crowd behind me into the little porch, sniffing eagerly. We would push open the door and look in to see my aunt, fat and flurried, rushing around tending dozens of pots and pans all steaming with goodness.

"Walter, you take those mucky boots out of here and put them on the step!" she'd bark.

"See, I told you," I would whisper.

"You're too smart by half."

"Yours, too, Donnie!" Another bark.

"Yes, come on, Donnie, put 'em out," my uncle would repeat with mock severity and, under his breath, "Put 'em right on her big, fat fanny."

Pot roast it would be, or roast pork, or salt codfish and scrunchions, or baked haddock fresh from the wharf a mile away, or—my favourite—a huge steaming steak and kidney pie. And always with lovely, warm, freshly-baked homemade bread and sunny vegetables straight out of the garden. For dessert, hot cherry or apple pie with rich hours-old cream and then steaming-hot strong tea.

The milk had a smell to it the like of which you never find today, the butter was rich and bright yellow, the preserves somehow tastier and sweeter, the pickles crisper and tarter, and, with the appetite I could work up in those days, none of it stayed around for too long. -

One suppertime we were having fresh mackerel and my father was present on one of his very rare trips to the country. As he chewed the deliciously doughy bread and forked the flaky flesh in between his old yellowed teeth, he I remarked on the hardships of the fisherman.

My uncle, not knowing what he was in for, called them "the farmers of the sea."

My father was instantly indignant. "You speak for yourself," he said harshly. "But don't drag those poor labouring men into your bourgeois circle."

"Now, now, Tom," said my aunt, "Walter's right. They're just like us: in business for themselves and what they get out of it depends upon what they put into it."

"In business like Old Harry," my father erupted, bits of food spraying from his mouth. "Those fishermen are labour, like me!"

"Well, Tom, you couldn't put us into that bracket, now could you?" my uncle asked seriously.

"Why not?" Daddy bawled. "Think you're so goddamned special? You people make me sick with your noses in the air. You get a few acres of dirt, make a miserable few hundred dollars a year, and you think you're aristocracy. Businessmen! *Pahh*!"

"Don't deny it, Tom."

"Deny it? Of course I deny it. Do you have any control over your prices? No! Do you have any control over your taxes? No! Do you have any control over the cost of your feed? No! Machinery? No! Can you sell where you like? No! Can you rear what you like, grow what you like? No, you're dependent upon the 'market forces.' And who sets the market forces? Eh?

Tell me that, Mr. Businessman? Is it you? Is it any of you dirt scratchers? No! Why, Walter, b'y, in some ways you're worse off than I am. All you can boast about is a nice place to live and a healthy environment."

"That will do, Tom," my aunt said sharply.

"Oh, well, all right, May," he grumbled, then continued to mutter, "Petty bourgeoisie...reactionary forces...can't rely on the peasantry."

Uncle Walter was a Tory—a "black Tory," as my father put it—and occupied an executive position in the local constituency association. At election time he drove his wagon and later his truck to pick up voters and take them to the polls. He also took charge of the rum which would be distributed around the farms and fishing villages to show the voters how magnanimous the party could be.

Uncle Walter could predict within three votes the results in the four polls of which he was in charge. It was simply a matter, he said, of subtracting the dead and adding those who had come of age. The reason he could not predict with greater accuracy, he told me, was because there were three "ornery, foolish MacRae brothers" who sometimes did not vote at all and when they did, never voted the same way twice in a row.

I remember asking him if any of the others ever changed their vote and he looked at me in absolute horror.

"What?" he sounded incredulous. "Just as well ask a man to change his religion or disown his own father."

After supper was over I would sit at the window, my elbows on the sill, chin in hands, and stare out into the gradually darkening sky. Slowly, the clouds would turn grey-purple with cream edges, then blend in together, leaving only a narrow strip of lightness on the horizon. The hills would grow deeper green and, as the light, patchy fog began to drift in, they would become a uniform black, grim and brooding, shouldering the little farm into the spreading gloom.

Then I would go into the cozy front room, with its quaint old furniture and great grill in the floor where the heat came up, and curl up in a big armchair and listen to Uncle Walter tell tales.

What tales they were! To my young ears, they were tales of courage and death, battles, great treks across barren lands, tales of honour and romance. In reality, Uncle Walter was giving me history lessons (and surprisingly accurate ones I later discovered), but painting this history with broad strokes and vivid colours to catch the imagination and coax the memory to retain them.

He spoke of the Battle of Culloden in which his forefathers fought and in which many of them were killed by Cumberland's soldiers. He spoke of the barbaric Highland clearances in which their graces the Dukes of Sutherland and Argyle deemed it more profitable to turn the beloved glens over to Cheviot sheep than let them remain in the charge of coarse, ignorant crofters. So they hired Englishmen and the hated lowlanders to come with guns and pikes and drive the highlanders from their cottages.

The black cattle, the symbol of life, disappeared, and the cottages were burned, the women kicked and beaten, and the men killed or jailed. They drove them to the coasts, where many were herded aboard rotting and disease-ridden hulks, and others left to learn to fish from the black, inhospitable rocky shores.

Many of those who had the few pounds to try the hulks came here to Cape Breton, where their line continued to fight the taxes and the weather. Such a man was Uncle Walter, a Fraser, descended from those who wandered across Caithness, hungry, cold, and diseased, until they reached the sea and staggered on board a ship bound for Pictou. Thousands came to the New World, thousands more perished.

My uncle told me that when the priests and recruiting sergeants travelled the Highlands to find volunteers to fight in the Crimea, they found but a few miserable specimens. When they gathered at Dunrobin, not far from the Duke of Sutherland's estate, Uncle Walter said, a delegation approached the officials and told them that since they had preferred sheep to men, sheep could defend them and fight their battles.

Now they are all here, digging coal in Glace Bay, fishing in Richmond, farming in Margaree, logging in Victoria, all mixed up not knowing, for the most part, who they really are nor where they came from. But it is clear that most of the great clans are represented.

MacDonalds by the thousand: MacDonalds of Sleat, Clanranalds, MacEans of Glencoe, MacNeils from everywhere to everywhere, and many of them; MacLeans, MacLeods from Skye and Mull, MacIntoshes, MacGilivrays, MacAulays, Frasers, Rosses, MacEwans, MacIvers, and, of course, the fated Campbells who, it would seem from history, had no reason to flee their homeland, but are here anyway to share this little island.

"Be careful what you say, now," Aunt May would chide. "You'll give the boy nightmares."

"Not a bit of it," Uncle Walter would reply, winking at me and sucking on his pipe.

He was wrong. When curled up in the rickety, noisy bed, listening to the wind and rain shake the window-pane and the old roof creaking, the images of MacEan being slain in his nightshirt by the bloodthirsty Glenlyon would come sweeping into my mind and carry me off into sleep on a wave of gory dirks, slashing claymores, flying kilts, and moans of pipes over the smoking cottages of my ancestors.

Times with my grandparents were different. While interesting, they were not as exciting. The days seemed softer, more mellow, the breezes more gentle, the waters warmer. There, not far from Iona, in the middle of the lakes, I swam day after day, lazed in the orchard, fished with my grandfather's rod, and looked up at the blue sky, chewing stalks of grass.

There in that mellow land lie my very fondest memories: the long, hot days when I would take

Poppy's boat out into the shining waters and lay back with my hands trailing in the cool, lapping waves; the quiet, almost solemn evening meals across the table from two old people, growing more lovely as time passed; the beautiful little bays where rich green spruce grew right into the clear water; the smell of summer so heavy over us while we sipped cold lemonade underneath the elm tree; the knowledge that coal and company, death and hardship, rum and rowdyism were a whole world away.

Poppy told stories too, chiefly ghost stories. He was not as quick or as colourful as Uncle Walter, but took his time, picked his teeth, and casually, gruffly, spun his incredible yarns like timeless thread over my senses.

There was the story about the ghost ship which silently slipped up the lake, anchored just out from the shore and sent a dory bearing four men with shovels and an old lady in a sedan chair. They carried her for about half a mile, so the legend goes, at which point she instructed them to start digging.

After an hour's work, the men hauled from the hole a huge oaken chest which was placed in the sedan chair alongside its occupant, both of which were then transported back to the ship in the manner in which they had come. Then the ship lit a single lantern, quietly weighed anchor, and slipped away through the night.

Unbelievable as it was to me then, today it is ludicrous, but I swear that my grandfather had no doubt whatever that it was true. So it was with all his stories; the fact that he related them with such sincerity and conviction made them all the more enjoyable to the attentive listener.

9: Red-faced plumpkins

Agincourt Cresc.

Dear Ma and Daddy,

Tom and me was surprised about Daddy's birthday. We never thought he was that old!! I guess you'll be after thinking about how you will both spend your days now and I know Ma is getting sick and tired of all the dirt and wind at the old Dump.

Tom and me was thinking the other day and Tom suggested we ask you to come up here and live with us. We got lots of room here and the kids are grown up enough not be bothering Da with a lot of noise when he's reading the paper. We know you'd love it here and we're right close to the bus stop so you can ride into town to shop and look at the lights any time you like. We've got our own shopping centre just a few blocks away and the A and W just built a new place right around the corner (Tom likes the Teenburgers and the kids are wild for that Chubby Chicken). Da can go down to Queen's Park and watch the politicians beat their gums and Ma you can play bingo every night up at the church and the back garden is nice sit out in and soak up the sun.

Will could take the house and we know he wants to get hitched pretty soon and its hard to find places when you're first setting up. Lord knows he has been waiting long enough.

Let us know as soon as you make up your minds as Tom wants to build an extension to the end of the house if he can get the planning permit or something. Tom and the kids send their love. Me too.

Ruby

Split-level, pebble-dashed, white-trimmed, car-por-ted, corner-lotted, asphalt-fringed, semi-circled re-tirement haven for worn out, beaten down, grubby old coarse-tongued working-class radical. The great T.O. Hogtown. Concrete Utopia. Centre of the civil-ized world. Rose-bushed suburbia. Brand new street lighting, regular police patrols, sparkling curb and gutter, *cul de sac.*

Sit in the back garden, she said, and soak up the sun. Doesn't she know that I have been to Toronto in January? Has she forgotten that I lived there after the war?

What is wrong with my own back yard? The fence needs painting, I know that, and that pile of old cans and tires is none too pretty, but the sun shines here too. High pressure salesmen, that is what they are.

How convenient to live near the bus stop. Look at the lights, she said. If I want lights I can walk up onto our hill and look across the water to Glace Bay. Yes, but they are not moving lights, I can almost hear her argue, but I would sooner sit on the can out back and run my flashlight up and down the fence.

Wall to wall carpet, Marg tells me, it is like walking on air and the children will be very quiet. I never met a quiet child in my life, and if I want to walk on air I can just stand up and step off this cliff.

The sea is beautiful today, a nice, bright pea-green in spots where the light shines through onto those flat, light-coloured rocks underneath. God knows I shall miss this if I give in to them.

Where can you see a sight like this in Toronto? I used to wander around the lake there and never saw such filthy stuff in my life. Damn few gulls, too.

Maybe it is just stubbornness on my part to go against the wishes of the whole family, but I cannot see myself getting excited over Chubby Chicken and bingo just around the corner. I have never bowled, so their spanking new fifty-lane Bowlerama will not do me much good. I wouldn't mind having a sit in on Queen's Park, but compared with the local it would be kid's stuff.

It is not that I am ungrateful for Ruby's offer, but it sounds like the kind of place where they'd be ashamed to hang out their washing and where the kids would be chained up and the dogs fitted with silencers. I am sure I would never see a drunk on Agincourt Crescent, and would certainly never see Crooked Billy hobbling down the row full of spittle and gossip.

Oh, God, and what about the bells on Sunday? You need a certain kind of sea mist for church bells to sound right, and I never heard that sound in Toronto or anywhere else away from the ocean.

I read the letter again and sure enough that young bugger is trying to put his father out of his own life-long home so he can get Annie Pyke in there. Of course, he did not come to me and tell me he wanted to get married soon and would like the house.

Why doesn't she tell the Pykes to leave their place?

If he had told me I would have cleared out quickly and tried to get one of those rentals they are building for senior citizens over in Glace Bay. He had to go behind my back, writing to his sister to engineer a plot to lure me to Toronto. I guess I cannot really blame him because a miner's life is hard and he cannot afford to buy a home.

He could have told me instead of beating around the bush.

Anyway, I decided to give him a run for his money the day the letter came.

"Ma tells me our Ruby wrote today," he'd said casually as he came down from washing after work.

"That's right," I said, equally offhand.

"Did she have anything interesting to say?"

"Kind of."

"Yeah? What'd she get to say then?"

"Oh, you know what her letters are like. All about the concrete jungle." I was getting malicious enjoyment out of keeping him on a string.

"Ma said something about you two moving up there. That right?"

"No!" I said firmly, rolling myself a smoke with my old ZigZag.

"Oh." He looked disappointed. "I thought Ma wanted to go."

"Yes, your Ma wants to go, but there's nothing definitely settled yet. We'll need some time to think on it." I stuck the cigarette in my mouth and lit up, puffing vigorously in his direction.

Will walked to the window and affected an interest in something going on down at the bottom of the row. He leaned on the ledge and peered out for a few minutes, then straightened up and turned around, trying to look very serious.

"Da, do you think I should get married?"

How the Christ do I know? I thought to myself, I'm hardly the ideal one to be giving advice on that subject, but you can't say that to your son even if he is trying to put you out on the street.

"If you want to. What's stopping you?"

"I've been thinking about it for a while now," said he, stroking his chin like a professor of psychology.

"Oh? Anyone in particular?" I asked, teasing him along.

"Well, there's Annie."

"A good girl," I said with an appreciative wink.

"Sure, sure. But I don't know. Everything's so dear. To build a house now on today's pay is nigh impossible."

"Well, you'll have to rent for a while. It's quite usual for newlyweds."

He gave up, flapped his arms like he usually does when he is frustrated, and stalked into the kitchen where I heard him muttering to his mother. The hissing of all those sweating pots and kettles drowned him out and only when I heard the gate clattering did I realize he was gone.

Takes a bit of imagination to see my Will married off, and at his age. He's older than I was when Marg finally nailed me down, and I didn't think he'd ever get around to it.

Sure, I knew he was seeing Annie Pyke, but I thought he was going to be like Freddie Johnson who courted the same woman for thirty-five years and didn't marry her yet; Freddie still lives up the top of this row and Ethel still lives in her mother's old place.

So the bug has bitten Will and he wants to marry Annie Pyke, and the pit, and this town, and my house. Well, he's a much more steady type than I ever was and he's not much interested in books or travelling or politics and, God knows, maybe he's the better off for that.

One thing we do have in common is the fact that we both want to live right here in Cape Breton. Marg sees this place as a prison, but not me. And not Will. We're here by our own choosing and supposing I do like to trot around once in a while, I always come back here. To this grubby little town at the edge of the world. To this cliff, too. Now I think of it to the very same spot by this old rock and that patch of clay where the grass will never grow.

Well, I hope to Jesus his marriage will be better than ours. Not that there haven't been good times, but it never really clicked. The head-shrinkers always talk about "working on a marriage" and "talking things out," and such like stuff the very thought of drives me near crazy. She's no martyr but she deserved better than the likes of me.

I could blame it all on the Trap, but that would be too easy and unfair. There is no question that the way things were around here from time to time would drive a progressive man to distraction, but I will accept responsibility for my own actions.

It is indeed a wonder that she never left as Ma had once left Daddy, and I often came home from one of those early, salty jaunts expecting the house to be empty, but it never was. The soft, warm light falling on the pathway, and the tender, ever so slightly stale kitchen smells on the air outside the back door were so welcoming as to fill a man with quiet to the bottom of his boots. To be sure, she gave the rough of her tongue many's the time, but I swear she understood what it was that drove me away.

"I can see I'll have a job keeping you home, my man," she'd said with a bright, sparkling laugh as we stood arm in arm at the wedding reception.

I grinned all right, but I think even then I was itching to be away roving or playing the fool, thinking of Jeanette.

What a wedding it was! The boys had filled me with every kind of liquor under the sun. Everett Mac-Adam was my best man and Marg's parents were there looking for all the world like a historic photograph, starch stiff, tut-tutting, and continually sniffing as if they were trying to locate a dog's business.

All the shining, freshly scrubbed, red-faced plumpkins came to say goodbye to Mr. Single, eating their melting hearts out, at least so I told myself, and Daddy hovering around looking like a director of BESCO in his best suit. Multi-coloured streamers in the old church hall, Blind Mat on the accordion, Uncle Archie falling all over Mrs. Blinkhorn and Ma, alone in the corner, a blackened stump after the lightning had struck.

Poor Ma! She has been dead many a year now and it was always a mystery to me why she and Marg disliked each other so much. What donnybrooks they used to have, each blaming the other for my errant ways, the prosecution indicting the judge for the defendant's crime. Daddy, like a good many other fathers before him and since, said that two women could not live in the same house without fighting and, by God, it was certainly true in our house.

What was most unfortunate was that the children were often used as foot soldiers in the war between the women.

Of the two, there is no question that Marg was the closer to me and the more understanding. She even voted my way, something my mother never did to her dying day—much to the disgust of Daddy who said that she was "ruining" his ballot.

I can't recall now how I first got around to courting Marg, but I think it was probably through her brother Collie. I used to hang about with him in the early thirties and I guess I must have noticed her at his place on one of my visits. I had broken up with Jennie MacIntosh just after the strike because I still clutched to hopes that Jeanette would reappear out of the blue. So it was that for a couple of years I had nothing to do with women but, as some of the pain started to fade away, I began to listen to the voices in the family circle-the same kind of talk I've been hearing about Will from Marg and Ruby.

"Lord bless us," I heard Ma say to Daddy one day when I was sitting on the back step, "I don't know what we are going to do with the man, Tom."

"Donnie's all right, my dear, just leave him be for a while."

At the sound of my name my ears perked up and I shuffled my rear end a little closer to the crack in the door. They say that eavesdroppers never hear anything good of themselves, but even those who believe it still want to lap up every word.

I sneaked a glance through the crack and saw Ma peeling spuds at the sink and tossing her head the way she always did. I could only see Daddy's boots and the corner of the newspaper he was reading.

"The man's over thirty years of age," Ma snapped back. "He can't go on living at home like a young pup all his life."

"Don't worry, woman, there's worse things could happen."

"It's all very well for you to sit there saying 'don't worry', but there'll be people thinking there's something wrong with the boy. My heaven, Tom, at his age you and me already had four children."

"It doesn't do for everybody to be alike," grunted Daddy, rustling his newspaper to indicate he thought the conversation should end as soon as possible.

"I thought for a while he was going to marry the MacIntosh girl from Morien, but it just sort of faded away. It was the strike that did it," she said bitterly, seizing a fresh opportunity to condemn Daddy's union activities. "Damn strikes, all they ever do is cause trouble and strife."

"Dear God, what next?" my father murmured quietly to himself.

Ma was clattering a saucepan so she did not hear him, and rattled right on. "It's not as if there was a shortage of young women around here, Tom. My Lord, there's dozens. Take that nice Ginny McCuish up on Seventh Street. Just right for our Don."

"Is that the skinny one with the intelligence of a blackfly?" Daddy enquired and I silently cheered him on. Ginny McCuish! My mother's ideas of nice women were markedly different from my own.

"You can sneer and scoff all you like, Tom Ross, but let me tell you that pretty soon he'll be too old to get anyone but the old maids, like Hester Campbell."

"Good God, woman," my father exclaimed, "what

world are you living in? The last thing I should call Hester Campbell is an old maid, and if you don't know why then I'm not about to tell you."

I almost laughed out loud. Hester Campbell was a well-known prostitute who practised her trade in town but who lived at the top of our street, neat as a new pin in a nice little house with a rose garden in front. Having known Hester very slightly over the years I could have told Ma she was definitely preferable to Ginny McCuish.

"You're always sneering at everything I have to say, Tom. You always did. I know you think I don't know nothing and that I'm just an ignorant country woman and that's why I don't understand your precious union and go along with your trashy strikes and godless politics, but I tell you something's got to be done about that man."

"What do you want me to do?" Daddy threw down the newspaper at his feet. "Go knocking on every door in the row asking if there's anyone inside wants to marry our Donnie, then drive the pair of them at gunpoint down to Father Ranald?"

"Talk to him, Tom," she said quietly. "You're his father. Why don't you act like it for once?"

"All right," he sighed. "But I can't guarantee results."

I nipped smartly down from the step and around the house to the front gate where I suddenly made a noisy show of fixing one of the hinges.

Daddy's face appeared in the window and within seconds he was coming towards me, his slippers shuffling among the weeds in the pathway. He stood watching me for a while, then pulled out his pipe and lit up.

"Your mother and me have just been talking," he said between clouds of smoke.

"Oh, yes?"

"Yes," he said staring at the gate. "There's nothing wrong with that hinge, Donnie. What are you after clouting it for?"

"Just to make sure of it."

"Here, let me have a look," he said brushing me aside. "Perfect. Strong as can be. What the hell's going on?"

"Keep your voice down, Da," I said. "I wanted to make sure Ma didn't know I just came from the back step."

"Ah." Recognition dawned on his face and the pipe lay along his chin. "Then you—?"

"Yes. Tell her you gave me a good talking to and that I'm looking into the possibilities."

"Thanks, b'y," he said, obviously relieved. "You know that as far as I'm concerned—"

"Yeah. I know, Daddy."

"Well, I best be going back inside then," he said, jawing the pipe to the horizontal position, squinting up at the wispy herringbone clouds and giving me a light punch on the arm. "And do a good job on that hinge now."

Well, that set me thinking. When I started to look around there were almost none of my contemporaries who were still single; the exceptions were either alcoholics or simpletons and one or two others who were queers.

While I had no great desire to get married, neither, I found on examining myself, did I have very much against it. I guess that when I had hung around Collie MacPhee's house a few times and had noticed the twinkling red-haired sister with the tight little chest pushing at her white blouse, I thought to my-self maybe it was time to win some credits in Ma's book.

It was not that I actually planned on going the whole hog and getting married, but that I could have a bit of fun and keep on Ma's good side at the same time. I had been after disgracing myself on a couple of dandy bats on the pop and Ma had been giving me the frosty glare, so I needed something to restore the balance of normal relations in the house.

Truth to tell, I had heard one or two stories about Marg, the kind she would not want her mother to hear—but it did not bother me. I was never much for putting stock in gossip nor in judging other people's morals, and, to be honest, I was half hoping they were true.

She was a mischievous little vixen, full of sparkle, fire, and tease, but warm as her blood may have been, she certainly did not live up to her reputation because I found her as strict and as straight as could be. I used to kid her by telling her she was as stuffy as her parents, and when I did she didn't know whether to laugh or hit me.

Lord, what a weird pair of creatures they were. I

had never met anyone as puritanical and as boring as Mr. and Mrs. MacPhee—they even called each other "Mr." and "Mrs." and the children had to call them "Father" and "Mother." They went to church about five times a day, I think, and did not allow books, newspapers, or a radio into the house.

Arnold MacPhee always wore a stiff white collar and tie, no matter what time of day or year, and Agatha was always done up to kill in black and lace. He was a clerk with the town and was very much against drink, gambling, dancing, music, sport, and adultery. Agatha agreed with everything he thought.

Lucky for all of us they never breathed a word about politics or union affairs, otherwise Marg's and my courtship would have been off very early on in the game.

In view of the kind of parents they had it was miraculous that Marg and Collie were so outgoing and saucy, and we had some great old times together, Marg and me, and Collie and his girl Annie-May. In fact, we did all the things Mr. MacPhee was against-except the adultery-and were all the better for it.

I even managed to win Marg over to the cause of the union and to progressive politics. We used to sit up on the grassy bank above the reservoir and discuss the issues of the day; me spouting and gesticulating like a revival preacher and Marg, head tilted, eyes shining, her tight little red curls burnished by the evening sun, and her lovely chest straining away at the dazzling cotton.

I think it was the fascination with her chest that

prevented me from holding out any longer than I did, for after we had been going out together for less than a year, I asked her to marry me and she accepted.

The wind was whistling along the rows, throwing the trees into confusion, and scattering the red and brown leaves all around us. Papers and bits of boxes skittered along the fences and the dry, yellow grass was almost bent flat. The smoke was being snatched from the chimneys and hurled in all directions. The sea was dark grey with little whitecaps littering its surface, and Marg's hair was blown straight back from her face, revealing her two delicate white ears.

"I guess you know what you're getting yourself into," I said.

"I have an idea," she smiled. "I'm not deaf, you know. I've heard some of the stories about you."

"My God, what did you hear?"

"Never you mind, my boy. There's some of them I wouldn't have the gall to repeat. But I'll tell you this, there's none of them good!"

"Malicious gossip is what it is, girl. Anyone around here can tell you I have led the life of a monk."

"Monk, is it?" She laughed into the gust. "A defrocked monk, then!"

"Listen, Marg," I drew her close to me, "I'm serious now. You don't know the kind of person I am. Restless and rootless. You're letting yourself in for a handful of trouble is my guess. And you know how I like a drop of rum now and then."

"Well, we'll just have to get you some roots fast

and keep you away from the Black Diamond. I'll take my chances."

I wonder now if she wished she had heeded me on that windy October afternoon so many years ago. She knows now that I certainly was not exaggerating hen I warned her I was a bit of a rascal.

Mind you, she's not exactly an angel and she has a tongue on her with an edge Mr. Gillette would have paid a fortune for, but there is no question she has had the worst of the deal.

I don't know why Ma hated her. I had started courting Marg to worm my way back into Ma's good books and when I told her I was bringing Marg home, I thought she would go crazy with delight.

Daddy was charmed off his feet—no matter what he may have said later—and was shambling around like a teenager trying to make Marg feel at home.

Ma took one look at her and the ice came into the harbour two months early. She never said a word against Marg to me, but from the moment they first laid eyes on each other it was war to the knife.

"Well, Ma, what do you think?" I asked her after I had followed her out to the kitchen to get the tea.

"A man's waited as long as you have can't afford to be choosy," she said, rinsing the pot under the tap.

"Jeez, Ma, is that all you've got to say? I thought you'd be pleased."

"Donnie, you'd have to get married sooner or later. It wouldn't be natural if you didn't."

At first, of course, I could not afford a house and for a few years we all lived together. Daddy had a chance to buy the other half of the company house so we had more room, but it was still a living hell.

Marg and Ma were sniping at each other day in, day out, and I'm glad that we had moved out before Daddy died because often he was all that stood between an armed truce and outright slaughter. It was as if they improved each other's powers in the process of the civil war, sharpening their minds upon the other's insults, and finely honing their sarcasm till it could draw blood.

"Oh, Marg, dear, would you mind not putting washing in the sink just before dinner time. Tom likes to eat off a clean plate occasionally."

"Why, Ma, I thought the plates would be cleaned after breakfast."

"When a woman has to do so much of the work without help, she doesn't have the time to always do what should be done."

"Now I would have thought a smart woman would have planned out her time ahead to avoid getting into a mess all the time."

"Messes caused by others, no doubt. Carrying the burden for others is something I'm quite used to."

"I hear God places the burdens upon the beasts best able to bear them."

"Marg MacPhee, are you calling me an ass?"

"Ma, dear, what gave you such an idea? But if you're after thinking the hat fits, why not wear it?"

"My Lord, in the country, where I was brought up, such insulting behaviour was unknown, I'll tell you."

"If it was so good in the country, why did everybody leave it?"

Even if it was tough to live with, I must give Marg credit for being the only one I know who could stand up to Ma and not be driven into submission, silence, or retreat. She could give as good as she got all right, and sometimes Daddy and I would just sit back in the front room and enjoy the show.

"Marg, *dear*, you know my mother always told me you should only hold a cup by the handle."

"Did she now, Ma, *dear*? Mothers are full of advice, aren't they now? Mine told me how ignorant it was to even mention such things."

"Yes, that's true, *dear*, but my mother told me there are some serious cases where you have to make an exception."

"Yes, *dear*, so did mine—country people and them's is a bit weak in the head, y'know."

We did have some good times, Marg and me; some funny, some tender, some priceless. God knows how much longer we've got left together before we mingle with the coal dust and the bones of those that are already gone. There's no sense in fooling yourself about these things; it will be inside ten years that they'll be lowering me into a brown hole up in Raines Road Cemetery and Marg'll be following close after.

I guess a fellow would be smart to make the best of what's left. She was always there. I guess I owe her something. Maybe this is my way of repaying her. Maybe I will go to her pristine subdivision. Just for her.

10: Stiff and black with sorrow

There is no other experience quite like standing in the semi-wilderness of a catholic graveyard, listening to the strains of detached chanting being snatched by the breeze, a sentence here, a verse there. Each occasion feels as if it is merely a continuation of the last, as if no time had elapsed. Feet uncomfortably planted in the tangle of last year's dead grass, mourners would stand dotted around the barren hill like chess pieces, placed by a hand which would also be needed if they were ever to move again.

Tight, irritating collar pinching freshly-scrubbed and shaved-pink skin; the stiff, salty wind ruffling carefully slicked down hair; the slight, soft smell of wild sage drifting on the breeze; the rustle of the stunted shrubs around the legs; the quiet, muted drone of the prayer; the sharp, rasping noises of the bereted pallbearers easing their burden; deep, deathly silence eventually broken by the desperately forlorn bugle, thin and reed-like, its notes wailing, trailing into the whistle of the wind; a stifled sob followed by a low murmur gradually spreading over the hill.

These were the sensations of death.

Once, I dropped my strangely clean hand to the stunted bush by my side and plucked a leaf from the quivering branch. I lifted it to my face, and crushing it between my fingers smelled the sweet, new sap. The priest muttered something to the sky and I looked at the damaged leaf and asked, "What are we doing here?"

The answer came swiftly and purposefully: "Ssh-hhh!"

Before the hill, the church, chilling and sombre, creaking with sanctity, groaning with piety, filled with ornate mystery and all under an unfinished roof. While mothers and daughters sobbed and fell on each other's shoulders, the funeral mass would drone on and on, and the repeated reminder that all those who believed in Him would not die at all seemed to do little to reassure those affected.

I often wondered why it was that the priest did not memorize the mass instead of reading it and in so doing make it sound lifeless, cold, and empty. Up and down, kneeling, standing, sitting, glancing around to see who was sober, and always the tooth-less old lady who made a hobby out of funerals, and always the Canadian Legion, poppy stiff, blue, erect, and beribboned.

Before the church, the wake, dingy and grotesque, cruel in its duration and atmosphere. People became parodies of themselves when they entered the rest-ing room, held their hands unnaturally in front of them, deepened and muted their voices, and moved like zombies. The focal point, hundreds of dollars' worth of quilt, silk, teak, brass, flowers, perfume, cosmetics; the incredible and bizarre paraphernalia of ritual.

On the darkened and musk-smelling fringes, the semi-circle of seated relatives would nod silently as a mourner shuffled forward to kneel and bow his head. When I did it, I never knew what to look at, for to close my eyes seemed stupid and to stare at the lifeless, pallid, artificially serene face seemed indecent.

After crossing himself, the mourner would slowly rise and turn to the next of kin, muttering a halting, fumbled combination of time-honoured formulas.

"Umm...so sorry...fine man...er...anything I can do...er, let me know..."

"Sudden...why only yesterday..."

"Looked so good...terrible loss...who would have thought?"

"Er...well...I...er...must...have to be going...er...good-bye."

Then escape into the hallway where the air was cleaner, hastily scribble one's name in the gilt-edged visitors' book, and away to the world of the living: never was there such relief.

One wake I will never forget. It was held in a house down in the Glory Hole district and the neighbours were shuffling in and out to pay their respects to Fred Horner's wife, who had been struck down by a horse and cart on Main Street.

I passed in by the drab wreath hung outside the

door and ducked into the gloomy front parlour. There, surrounded by flowers, was the casket, its upper lid showing Mrs. Horner's face against a background of white silk.

At the door to greet me was the deceased's mother, stiff and black with sorrow. At her side, her husband, tall, erect, dignified. Around the room were the sisters and brothers, all gaunt and sober, their faces lengthened by the gravity of the situation.

You could cut the air with a knife and it felt like stepping into the grave itself. I mumbled a few words to the mother, who answered me in hollow, sonorous tones.

I nodded to the others and was making towards the casket when I saw the kitchen door burst open. It was Fred. He was wearing his pit boots, his work pants, and a filthy, wrinkled sweatshirt. In one hand, he had a bottle of beer, and in the other, a guitar. His shiny, bald head bobbed up and down, and when he saw me his face broke into a huge, toothy grin.

"Donnie, b'y!" he called out cheerily. "How's she going?"

"Not bad, Fred," I said in a hushed tone. "I'm sorry about your wife—"

"What? Ha ha! Don't be after worrying about her, b'y, she's happy," he chuckled. "Finally got clear of her after all these years. Come and celebrate!"

Never had I been so embarrassed in my life. Suddenly I was being asked to take sides in this morbid fiasco, incurring life-long hatred from one side or the other, depending upon which one I chose.

Fred grabbed me by the coat and pulled me towards the kitchen while the others frowned disapprovingly. I looked from one to the other, and finally succumbed to Fred's advances and followed him into the steamy, more cheerful, kitchen.

Perhaps it would be redundant to say that I got drunk, but ten o'clock in the night found Fred and me carousing along the clifftop singing "Nellie Dean" at the top of our lungs. Ashamed of it I am.

Another wake I attended with Dan Joe, and when we walked into the dim parlour the first person we saw was the Honourable Hector MacNally, our member of the legislature for ten years and formerly attorney general of the province. He had been defeated at the previous election by a Labour candidate and was now chief justice of the Supreme Court.

Earlier in the day, Jeff Beaton, Dan Joe, and I had raided the liquor store and, knowing that the honourable gentleman was partial to a drop, we decided to have some fun.

"Your Honour, would you care for a small drink of something?" Dan Joe asked, sidling up to him.

"Well, my good man," said MacNally, looking both ways, "that is uncommonly civil of you."

"If you care to accompany me out to the front door, I'll see what can be done."

We traipsed out onto the little front path and congregated there like three schoolboys sneaking a sly smoke.

"What is your preference, Judge?" I asked.

"Er... um... whisky...er—"

"No sooner said than done," Dan Joe cried, reaching behind the fence and coming up with a bottle of Johnnie Walker. He handed it to Judge MacNally, who accepted it gratefully.

"Are you not... er... drinking?" enquired MacNally.

"We prefer rum, Your Worship," said Dan Joe. "You can keep that bottle."

"Remarkably kind of you, I'm sure."

"Not at all, your Honour, we're only too happy to be of service."

At that moment we became aware of the siren, faint at first, then stronger as the police car approached our location. As the car screeched to a halt outside the front gate, Dan Joe and I whipped inside like a shot, leaving MacNally to face the law alone.

We put our ears to the door and could hear the exchange outside.

"Could I see that bottle?" the policeman asked.

There was some grunting and shuffling, then the young man spoke again. "I suppose you're going to tell me that you didn't even know that the liquor store was robbed today."

"The liquor store? Robbed? Why...er...no," MacNally stuttered. "Surely you aren't suggesting that I—"

"You're holding one of the bottles," said the cop. "Where did you get it?"

"From behind that fence...that is to say..."

A pause, followed by a clinking sound.

"Mmm-mm. And I guess you don't know that the rest of

the stolen stuff is behind that fence?"

"No, of course not." MacNally protested.

"But you just said that's where you got the bottle."

"Yes, I know, officer, but—"

"I think you'd better come with me down to the Town Hall."

"The T-Town Hall?"

"Yes, the police station."

"But you can't do that, my good man!"

"Oh, why not?" The cop was getting nasty.

"Because I am the chief justice of the Supreme Court of Nova Scotia," MacNally announced pompously.

"Well," said the policeman gently, "in that case I'll just take you down to the hospital."

That was as much as we could take without bursting into fits of laughter right in front of the corpse, so we withdrew to the kitchen and then hared away through the back yard.

We might have known, though, that MacNally would have the last word: Dan Joe was turned away at a number of places where he applied for a job; by sheerest coincidence I suddenly started getting the dirtiest jobs around the mine; and the young cop was fired.

It was often the custom with poorer families to get neighbours to dig the graves when someone died, and it seemed that Fiddler, Dan Joe, and myself were always roped in to perform the task.

One bitter winter's day, Little Reggie Cochrane died and his widow asked us if we would dig the grave. We went up the bleak, wind-swept hill, and started to hack away. The ground was so hard and frozen that by late afternoon we had still not finished.

Archie Warren, the undertaker, had brought up a rough casket and we pushed it down in the hole to see if it fit properly. Another two feet and the grave would have been perfect, but the others refused to continue without a drink to warm them up.

They turned away to town to get a bottle, but I stayed behind, having promised myself not to touch a drop until the weekend because I was missing so much work.

It was a dark, grey, miserable day, and the icy wind cut through my clothing, chilling me to the bone. The only visible refuge from the harsh weather was in the grave itself, so I got down into the box and pulled the lid over the top.

It was surprisingly warm inside and I must have waited like that for over half an hour before I heard the inebriated voices of my friends coming up the hill. Moving the lid a bit I could see the clouds tumbling angrily across the sky, and darkness was falling rapidly as they stumbled up to the graveside.

"Is that you, fellers?" I said, raising the lid and sitting up in the coffin. "What took you so long?"

Fiddler let out a screech which was closely followed by Dan Joe's ear-splitting cry. There was a frantic scuffle and away they went like rabbits on the moors. As I clambered out of the hole I could see them, a good quarter of a mile away, fleeing through the gathering dusk.

At first I thought it was funny, but when I had to finish the grave all by myself, I changed my mind.

Thankfully, Fiddler had dropped the bottle on the snow, so things could have been worse.

I forget the year, but it was shortly after a Bela Lugosi movie had come to town that Fiddler got the idea that there were vampires in Raines Road Cemetery.

"Vampires?"

"Are you crazy?"

"Now, listen, b'ys," Fiddler said seriously, his big, brown face close to ours, "there are more things in heaven and earth than are dreamed of in your philosophies."

"What's he talking about?" Dan Joe asked me.

"I don't know."

"Have a drink and I'll explain it to you," said Fiddler, passing a bottle of rum around.

By the time the bottle was empty, and he had finished relating the history and geography of Transylvania, every one of us firmly believed in vampires. Not only had Fiddler convinced us that they existed, but he had also decided on an individual.

"Who?" I asked.

"Who?" inquired Dan Joe.

"Who is it, Fiddler?" asked Shelly Gouthro.

"Norbert Blanchard!" Fiddler spat the name out.

"My God!"

"Jeeezus!"

"Is it not true, brothers, that the late Norbert

Blanchard was the meanest man who ever hung a pair of balls over a pisspot?" Fiddler asked, his eyebrows raised mysteriously.

We could not deny it.

"Is it not equally true, my friends, that Norbert Blanchard could only have been worse if he had been bigger...then there would have been more of him there to be rotten?"

"Right," said Shelly.

"Squeezed a quarter till the King shit in his hand," said Dan Joe.

"Didn't care if our Lord was crucified or killed with the Toronto shunt," said I, half-drunk and caught up in the melodrama.

"Well, then," Fiddler said darkly, "it is our sworn and solemn duty to liberate his soul and remove the menace from the face of the earth."

"How will we do that?" Shelly asked, his eyes bleary with rum.

"An ash stake," Fiddler whispered.

"Ash stake?"

"The only thing that will do it."

"There's no ash trees around here," I said. "Where are we going to find one?"

"It so happens," said Fiddler gleefully, as he snatched a broom from the corner, "that this object in my hand is none other than a piece of the very finest ashwood that money can buy."

"How?"

"Through the heart," said Fiddler.

"Where?"

"Raines Road," said Fiddler.

"When?" I asked.

"Tonight!"

About five hours and three bottles later, the four of us were stumbling up the hill towards the cemetery, Fiddler in the lead wearing a long, black raincoat, draped over his shoulders like a cloak. He brandished a small gilt cross in one hand to ensure "the protection of divine forces," he told us, and the broom in the other. We huddled close together, peering this way and that as we slowly came nearer the graveyard. -

"What's that smell?" Shelly asked.

"Garlic," Fiddler replied, holding up a handful of cloves tied in a pocket handkerchief he'd been carrying around for the occasion.

"Garlic?"

"What in Jeezname is that for?"

"They hate it."

"Who hates it?"

"Vampires hate garlic," Dan Joe cackled, hunching his back and making his hands like claws.

"Essential," Fiddler affirmed, "lest we be intercepted before our sacred mission be done."

Terrified beyond measure, we gathered around the spot which Fiddler assured us was the resting place of Norbert Blanchard. Fiddler took out a pocket knife and a mallet from his raincoat pocket and turned to us.

"Clear away the defiled ground," he whispered, "while I sharpen the stake."

We pulled away some rocks and cleared some of the soil. Fiddler crept forward, the stake in his left hand, the mallet in his right.

"'If 'twere done, 'twere well 'twere done quickly,'" he muttered, positioning the stake and raising the mallet high. "By the powers invested in me by His Excellency the Most High Emperor of Austria-Hungary, I dispatch this holy deed." His voice rose to fever pitch. "Death, where is thy sting?"

"What the hell's going on?" a man shouted from about fifty feet away. "Who's there?"

I never moved so fast in my life. I did not know where the others had gone, but I took off like the wind, stumbling over headstones, until I finally found refuge in a ditch at the bottom of the cemetery.

The only thing that joined me in the ditch was a bat.

~

I remember reading somewhere that in the midst of life we are in death, and it certainly seems to me that I spent a good third of my waking life attending funerals, wakes, and memorial services. Old men who died because they were downright tired of trying to struggle on in a household that did not want them; young men who choked to death trying to get that last precious breath of air; babies and children who simply wasted away because molasses and potatoes made their bones weak and their bodies soft; hard-working red-raw-handed women who were seized, screaming in childbirth, or who gave up the ghost while heaving a monstrous pile of washing up onto the corner post of the back yard fence; men of all ages—n sealed caskets—mangled beyond recognition, often in several pieces, victims of the coal they had spent their entire lives finding.

Amid the joyfulness and drunkenness and high-spirited loud living of our town-always death. Stiff as parchment and black as Sunday, a constant reminder that as bad or good as things were, they were but a very impermanent state of affairs.

The memorial services seemed to crop up with tedious regularity. Out would be trooped the medals, the berets, the poppies, the stiff dull-green artificial wreaths, and the titles: Zone Commander, District Commander, and all that stuff.

The regimental, brigade, battalion, company, and even platoon reunions which, while a grand excuse for a binge of roast beef, beer, and "Hang Out The Washing On The Siegfried Line," always had to be preceded by a service in which the heroic dead were remembered, honoured, eulogized, and possibly forgotten.

And in the shiny back rooms of hotels, the one-time officers—now professional smoothies who, as solicitors or business executives gouged their former charges worse than ever they did in wartime—staggered to their gentlemanly feet and offered toast after toast to "those grand chaps," the foot soldiers, without whom neither victory nor honour could have been possible.

I never ceased to be amazed by discoveries that some corrupt and mealy-mouthed official had once been a colonel or a major in wartime. These discoveries reinforced my opinion that in time of war our country had shown that it was even more desperate for leadership material than it was in time of peace.

I would sometimes go down and sit in the courtroom and watch Elroy Joseph, the magistrate, stumble and mutter over a simple point of law, and marvel at the fact that once this man had commanded a battalion. To amuse myself I invented situations in my mind wherein Elroy would be confronted with major decisions in the front line and while the enemy advanced a mile a minute, the incompetent would be crouched in a foxhole, hemming and hawing, and frantically thumbing through the pages of a military manual.

My daydream would climax when a private, coal dust still around his eyes, would quietly approach and casually point out to his C.O. the correct action to take. After the battle had been won, I pictured the ceremony where the mustachioed general pranced down the lines to award Major Joseph a Victoria Cross.

As the dream closed, the camera of my mind panned slowly down the lines until it came to rest on the private, unknown, unsung, standing stiffly to attention, his clear gaze fixed on a distant hill.

I have seen the sights of death, heard the many sounds of death, and of the rituals which followed it.

I have also smelled its stench-in the pit mixed with sweat, in my grandfather's room blended with bile, in the hospitals mingled with carbolic. Soon it will be my wake they will be attending and the Lord knows what eulogy I will get!

11: Neither chick nor child

Late May 1925, the strike was still deadlocked, and as far as I could see, nobody had a clue what to do about it.

Daddy's hope and enthusiasm never waned for an instant but I was near finished. I was sick to my soul for the hungry, the dead, the dying, exhausted by the endless talk and argument, and numb in the head from the propaganda war raging in the papers, on the streets, and in the taverns and union halls. If I had been skeptical of the strike at the beginning, I was now totally convinced it should be called off.

Yet, when forced to choose, I too would admit that while there was nothing to gain from fighting on, and maybe a great deal more to lose, we simply could not let Wolvin get away with it. Somehow we just could not give in to such a demon—his triumph would be too bitter for us to accept, his victory salt in our already infected and running wounds.

The realization that I was backing the wrong horse filled me with terrible depression and self-hatred. I rarely smiled now, and never laughed, and, when not doggedly, bitterly, mechanically carrying out my union duties, I would sit at the kitchen table drinking rum, if I could get any, and sinking deeper into gloom.

"For the love of God, put the bottle away, Donnie," Ma beseeched me late one night. "It was never the answer to anything."

"There's no goddamn answers anyway, Ma," I said, refilling the glass, "so what does it matter?"

"Don't blaspheme in front of me, child, or I'll give it to you with this broom!"

"All right," I said. "Don't be bothering me and I won't blaspheme."

"Somebody's got to be bothering you, Donnie. You're pining away here day after day. You don't see your father like that."

"He's a fanatic."

"He's that all right," she said ruefully, "although I don't like to hear you insult your father."

"It's no insult, Ma. I wish I could be like him."

"God forbid! You're plenty like him right now," she said, hurling the broom into the corner. "But at least it's better to be out and around than drinking your-self silly."

"Where is he, anyway?"

"He was away to Waterford with Angus MacEach-ern," she said, her tight, pink face shining under the lamp, and she sat down at the table. "Doing what, I don't know. He didn't tell me and I didn't ask. Strike stuff, I imagine. Is there anything else apart from strike and union?"

"Not much these days, Ma."

"Not much any day, it seems." Her little nostrils

quivered with indignation, her lovely hazel eyes flashing with righteousness. "What's wrong with doing a good day's work, minding your manners and your business, and going to church reg'lar and fearing the good Lord?"

"Ma," I said with a sigh, "there's no point in going all over it again. Can't you see I'm beat. Leave me be."

"Leave you be! How can I leave you be? You're my son!"

She leaned across the table and took my hand in hers. "Here you are, Donnie, twenty-five years of age with neither a chick nor a child, tearing your heart with black thoughts, and pickling your liver with rum. For heaven's sake, what's the matter, lad?"

"I feel like I'm finished, Ma. I'm tired of life."

"Will you listen to that. Tired of life! What you need is to settle down with a good woman. Are you still seeing Jennie MacIntosh?"

"Now and then, but it's not that, Ma. Even if it was I couldn't think of settling down now when there's no money coming in and the future so bleak."

"Well, blessed if I know what to do with you."

"Don't worry, Ma. Go to bed."

"What you need is a change," she said. "Yes, that's what you need."

"Oh, sure. And what kind of a change did you have in mind? Picket duty in Sydney Mines instead of the Dump?"

"Pickets! Pickets!" she snorted loudly. "The devil with them lot! I'll tell you what, Donnie, why don't you go visit your grandparents in Iona? The weather is nice and you could catch some fish and have a rest like."

"If it'll please you, I'll go."

"Please me. It's not to please me I'm asking for. I'm trying to stop you from going mad."

"Ma," I said, "I'll go Saturday. For a week or two. Now will you quit worrying and go to bed. I'll make Daddy his tea when he gets in."

"Are you sober enough to be making tea?"

"Good God, yes! I've only had three or four. I never got the chance to drink much more because you've been talking my head off here."

"All right, son, I'll leave you alone. I'll let Mother know you'll be coming next weekend. They'll be glad to see you."

I had agreed to go more to get rid of her than any-thing else, but as she pattered up the stairs and as she rhythmically said her beads in the room over my head, I got to thinking that a bit of a vacation in the country would not be half bad. I thought of the deep, cool, sweet-smelling woods, the dancing ceiling of rustling leaves, the blinding shafts of penetrating light in nature's cathedral, the gentle, pale sandy beaches, and the shimmering waters, and I thought there were worse things I could be doing with my time.

I pictured Gran and Poppy's neat little farm, set-tling into the verdant growth, overhung by the rich, shining shade trees, and radiating a profusion of flowers and vegetables in all directions, right to the edge of the forest on one side and to the pasture fence on the other. The docile and steaming golden-brown cows, forever chewing and staring, sticky spruce sap on my hands, pebbles under my feet, cool water between my toes, flies buzzing against the window-panes, the smell of apples in the front room, the haze on the hill, the mist in the creek, the birdsong in the morning.

Ma was a genius! I was going.

The very dearest memory of my life springs from the soft lake country when I visited Gran and Poppy that May. It has stayed with me throughout all the storms and struggles and fog of the years. It is the only precious gem I ever owned,

I would not have been without it for the world, and nobody could have taken it from me supposing they had cut me to pieces and dug into my very soul to find it. It is far dearer than anything I can remember of Marg and I have never told her. Even now it holds me fresh, gently lingering in body and mind alike.

I had left that Saturday, the fights and hunger behind me, trying to sort out in my mind what it was that we radicals were doing and in what direction we should head next. Poppy and Gran, delighted to see me as always, made ready the little white room, fed me until I could hold no more fresh country fare, and put me to bed on a feather mattress.

After I had lolled around the house and garden for a few days, I ventured along the lake and then into the woods, exploring some of the old farms that were deserted even at that early date. The telltale signs would be a clearing in the trees, then the odd apple tree, gnarled and barren, and intertwined with the small evergreens which pushed in on all sides. A rectangular hollow in the ground marked the collapsed cellar of the house.

Some houses would still be standing or rather leaning-against a small hillock, almost white with age and exposure, the shingles rotting and curling, the old doors hanging from rusty hinges, and faint traces of glass around the bottoms of the windows.

Inside they would be cool, dank and musty-smelling, usually with a tiny cloud of buzzing flies up in one corner. On the floor would be strewn old, faded wallboard, the occasional piece of broken crockery stamped "Lovecraft, Stoke-on-Trent," a page from a yellowed, ancient catalogue, and a thousand little bits of broken plaster, testaments to the efforts of a Scottish couple determined to carve a comfortable home out of the wilderness.

I was strolling up a slight hollow on one of these deserted properties, sniffing the wild thyme and feeling the springy mat of years of old winter grass under the new growth, when I saw her about a hundred feet away, almost waistdeep in the lush hay.

I cannot describe my feelings at that moment, but the only way I have ever been able to explain it is that it was like a prophecy suddenly coming true. She was just disappearing under a dark green fringe of foliage at the edge of the woods when I called out.

She did not seem very surprised to be hailed in the middle of nowhere because she turned slowly and held up her hand to shield her eyes from the strong sun. At first she did not move, but as I came nearer—almost running—she took a few steps forward, which brought her out from under the dark canopy into the field.

When I was a few yards from her I shuffled to a standstill, awkwardly clutching at the tops of the grass, wrapping it round my fingers. I simply stood and looked. She was the sort of girl you could not take your eyes off, the sort who, in a crowd, would keep your gaze involuntarily turning towards her, a girl you would know had gone from a place without having seen her leave.

It is difficult to recall my emotions, to describe what happened. I felt weak, awkward and very, very young. All my life I have been uncomfortable with women, except in the dark, never knowing the correct things to say, never knowing what to do with my hands and feet. Even with Marg I find it difficult to look her in the eyes for any length of time without feeling grubby and ill at ease. So it was with this girl; the first time, but not afterwards.

"Good day," I said finally.

"Good day," she said, clear as spring water.

"I... er... was just exploring."

"Exploring?"

"Yes. I mean, is this your land? That is, am I trespassing?"

"Nobody trespasses here," she said, "unless they're from the city come to disturb the birds or the animals."

"Well, I'm from the city, but I don't wish to disturb anything." I paused. "Am I disturbing you?"

"No."

"Good. Come and sit down," I said, amazed at my own boldness.

Her name, she said, was Jeanette MacLellan, and she was living or staying, I never found out which, on a farm not far away. Gently probe as I did, that is all I could discover.

She had the light Inverness lilt to her voice and the odd word of Gaelic regularly crept into her conversation. Some of the expressions I could understand, for I had picked up the language from my relatives, but most escaped me because the pronunciation was not the bastardized form I was used to. When I was stuck I told her and she translated as often as she could, but in many cases she would tell me there was no English equivalent.

She was, I judged, about twenty years old; though her ways were older. She had very long chestnut-brown hair, large hazel eyes, a wide red mouth, the corners of which quivered fascinatingly, and a slender, smooth neck, which was all but impossible to resist. She wore a long skirt of a material that swayed nicely as she moved and the cotton shirt she had tucked into her waistband covered a breathtaking bosom.

To say that I found her very beautiful would be to do less than justice to my mental and physical state. I was utterly smitten, dreams and worlds away, and my body was trembling. I could not believe it, but it was true and it was happening to me.

We talked for hours, there on that soft, sunny bank; I of the coal mines, my home and family, the bitter strike; she of the fields, lakes, trees, birds, animals, and flowers. We told each other of things with which we were familiar; she could tell me about the habits and haunts of the fox with the same degree of detail as I could describe the mannerisms of Jim and the comings and goings of the local union. They were two separate worlds and, in a way, each totally irrelevant to the other; our struggles in the coalfields, the hunger of the children, my dreams of a new world, had no bearing whatever on life there in the country. Her walks among wildflowers, by streams full of speckled trout, likewise seemed meaningless to the world of an industrial revolutionary.

Yet here both those worlds not only met and interlocked, but gave life to each other and became one.

That happened on the second day. We had arranged to meet on the bank where we had spent the previous afternoon. Strangely, we had set no time, but had just whispered "tomorrow" as we had parted.

When I arrived she was not there, so I wandered around the old property hoping to chance upon her kneeling by a clump of flowers or calling to a squirrel in a tree. I returned to the bank, sat down and waited, a terrible feeling of dread within me, fearing that she would not come. After a while, I don't know how long, hours or minutes, I lay back in the grass and closed my eyes against the sunlight.

No sooner had I done so than I felt her warm, soft hands gently pressing over my face. I could feel her smile on me and her soft hair tickling my face as she leaned over me. She took her hands away and as she placed them on my chest I opened my eyes and looked up at her, smiling smile for smile.

"You came so quietly," I said.

"Does the fox warn the partridge that he is coming?" she asked, her eyes laughing.

"No, but I'm not the partridge," I said. "I'm the fox and you're the vixen."

"Ah, we'll make a country boy out of you yet."

I laughed and turned over, pressing her down. Her expression suddenly changed, almost to one of pain.

"I love you," I said quickly.

"Donald, I love you," she said, as if she had not heard me and was making the first declaration.

"And I love you," I felt bound to repeat.

"Shhh! There's nothing wrong, Donald, don't look so worried. I won't eat you."

"It's not that," I looked down, puzzled, "it's just that..."

"I know, I know," she whispered more to herself than to me. "It's just that I like saying it. I love you."

She pulled me slowly down and I brushed her lips with mine, burying my face in her soft, sweet neck.

As her hands ran softly down my sides, I smelled her fresh hair, the new grass, the scented breeze, the flowers, and the hint of salt from the lake where the summer sun danced on the tiny waves as they gently lapped in and out over the clean, silver sand.

A young man's quick blood under a midsummer sky when nature drains the power from his brain and concentrates it in a short, throbbing lifeline is both a marvel and a folly. Even now, with extreme pain, I can feel the hot, wet creation on my hand and smell the incomparable warmness of a woman's joy.

And now, with tears in my eyes, as on many occasions before, I think that of this are real memories made.

For three glorious weeks, I lived the life of the first lover, springing over the green turf, breathing deep the refreshing smells of the season and, wherever I was, whatever I did, Jeanette was constantly on my mind.

Gran and Poppy thought I was ill, I ate that slowly and disinterestedly, or alternatively that I was crazy for staying out on the shores of the lake until three and four in the morning. Poppy pressed me little about my "condition," as Gran called it, so perhaps he knew or guessed what was going on.

I wondered if someone had seen us holding hands on the beach under the moon or coupled in that ultimate embrace in the grass, but if that had happened and he had been told, it did not worry me in the least. I was in love and did not care about anything.

One tender scene comes to me more often than the others. We were sitting on the sand right at the very edge of the water when she took my hand in hers.

"Your nails are black," she said.

"Yes, it's coal dust."

"Won't it come off?"

"With enough scrubbing, I guess, but it gets right underneath."

"I'll do it."

She placed my hands in the soft, warm water and gently rubbed my fingers with the fine sand, then, with short stalks of grass, she carefully probed under the nails, gradually removing the dirt.

So gentle and thorough was she at this task that I fell asleep, and when she woke me later she had my hands in front of me. They were not my hands, more like a lawyer's, because they were soft and pink with the nails shining clean.

"There, my miner boy," she said, smiling.

"Just like a woman's," I said, laughing. "Why did you do that? Because I'm too lazy to keep myself clean?"

"Keep them soft with me."

"Answer my question, Jeanette," I persisted.

"Because I love you and..." she turned her head away.

"And...?"

"And because your hands bring me alive," she said, her big eyes roving over my face. "So with every touch and every movement I want you to feel my life."

I simply nodded with absolute pleasure. There is nothing at all like the feeling a woman can give a man when she pays him a supreme compliment and tells him that she thrills to his touch. What swelling pride it brings and how big he feels, how tall, how strong, and how self-satisfied. It is a vanity with no fault, one time when a man need not be ashamed of being conceited.

With strength in my body and full up with love I led her, and was led by her, into a thousand delights. We slipped under the quiet, black spruce at midnight, the pine needles gently crunching underfoot. We ran along the sandy shores of the big lake and stood proud and naked on the wet rocks, our arms high above our heads, and looked at each other in the moonlight. We picked wildflowers and pushed them jokingly into each other's hair. We lay side by side in the sunshine and watched animals at work or play. And we made love.

Such love it was! Such that—terrible to admit—on my wedding night, I looked for the same heights of delight with Marg and forever in my marriage was disappointed when I did not find it.

Jeanette and I loved in the shallows of the warm water, splashing in our joy, we loved in old hay lofts, we loved in the long grass and on the low cliffs, we loved at midday and at night, sometimes under the moon and stars, sometimes under a low black canopy of night cloud, and, once, we loved out in an open field in the pouring rain.

Jeanette of my sunshine gave me a whole lifetime in those few weeks, which seemed as if they would never, could never, end. But they had to, for although I had no wish to do anything other than spend the rest of my life there in that warm place, my friends and comrades were hungry and one of life's battles was being waged without me.

"I have to go," I said quietly one day when we were sitting under the trees.

"Oh?"

"I'm secretary of the local and it isn't right that I should be away any longer."

"Do you have to go, Donald?"

"Yes, my love. You see it's my fight, one I helped to start, and one I should help to finish."

"When will the strike be over?"

"I don't know. It could be months."

"Months!" she cried, and I will never forget that cry.

"But I'll be back in two weeks—for the weekend."

"Yes?"

"Sure. I'll meet you at our farm, the one where we met, two weeks from Saturday. I'll travel out on Friday afternoon and see you there the next morning. Rain or shine."

"Sun will shine for us," said Jeanette, clasping me tightly and pulling me down on top of her. "It will always shine for us."

12: Goons!

When I returned from the country I found I had missed a great deal of action, but little with which I was not familiar. The odd beating in a darkened back street, the occasional break-in, ultimatums from the company matched by equally stiff announcements from the union, the death of a child from malnutrition, and endless, rowdy meetings in the streets and the union halls. It was as if I had never been away.

I could see it in the faces of the women as they hung over the fences and in the men as they gathered on the street corners, passing a cigarette around and grumbling to each other and, I fancied, even in the twitching faces of the bony dogs as they whimpered and sniffed for garbage.

The children showed it most of all, for worse than their pale, skinny look, their little faces, grubby with dirt, bore expressions of bewilderment. It was ironic, I thought as I strode down the station hill, that it always seemed that the victims of the struggle were those who not only could least understand it but had had no part in its creation.

Many of the drab company houses were closed and shuttered where the occupants had taken off for the country or more usually for relatives in Toronto. Some had pulled up roots entirely and made for the west coast to try to start a new life.

From halfway down the hill I looked out over the hazy rooftops of our town and the town beyond that. Only here and there was a wisp of thin, grey smoke climbing from a chimney-someone was burning a few shovelfuls of the precious bootleg coal.

The pitheads, tall and black, protruding from the maze of buildings like sentinels, were still and silent and the gates to the collieries were closed and pad-locked. The network of railways criss-crossing the town were deserted and quiet, their rails gleaming with the warmth of idleness. Even the traffic had disappeared from the streets, the horses and wagons, the trams and the bakers' carts had all been put away to rest in dark sheds.

The silence was broken only occasionally by the odd black motor-car loudly, brazenly, spluttering along, carrying government or company officials to some meeting or other. The nervous noise of the motor would fade and give way to the yapping of a dog or the murmuring of the wives in the back yards.

The atmosphere was like a coffee pot on the stove a few minutes before coming to the boil. Just when you think it will never boil, just sitting there, it begins gently hissing and quietly growling to itself.

So it is with a strike. When it seems that nothing will happen, something erupts, the steam rushes out, the pent-up energy flies in all directions, and then boils itself away to nothing.

On my second night home I sat draining my glass and dreaming about the soft fields and waters of the Bras D'Or when there was a thump on the back door.

I went to open it and there was Rory MacSween holding up my father, with Daddy's arm around his neck.

At first I thought the impossible had occurred—that Daddy had got drunk—but as they shambled forward I could see he was hurt. He was clutching his ribs with his left hand and on his cheek was a huge cut with a trail of blood oozing down his chin and under his collar. -

"Holy Christ! What in the Jesus has happened?"

"Help me set him down, b'y, there's enough time for tales later."

"Daddy, are you all right?" I asked as we dragged him over to the big rocker and put him into it. "For Jesus' sake who did this to you?"

"Goons," he groaned. "One bastard smashed me face with a truncheon and the other pounded me in the side with a big pole."

"Don't talk now, Tom," said Rory, pouring out a drink of rum and handing it to Daddy. "Get this down you and Donnie can be away to get Doc MacLellan."

"Hold your coal!" Daddy shouted, his face contorted with the pain. "You're going nowhere."

"Jesus, man, you got to see the doctor," said Rory.

"I got to do nothing," Daddy said testily, recovering some of his colour and much of his composure as he did so. "There's little wrong with me that a good night's sleep won't fix. Donnie, get some stuff to wash me down and see if you can sneak in and get my nightshirt without waking your mother."

"Right!" I said and was away up the stairs. I managed to grab the nightshirt and get outside the room, but the instant I closed the door I heard her voice.

"Tom?"

"No, it's me, Ma."

"Is your father home?"

"Yes Ma, he'll be up by and by. We're just having a bit of a chew and a cup of tea."

"Tell him don't be too late."

"Fair enough. Goodnight, Ma."

"Goodnight, son. God bless."

I went back down and put a finger to my lips to let them know to keep quiet until Ma had dropped off again. Then I sponged Daddy's wound, holding his head and him trying to back away from me.

It was a dandy cut, about five inches long, from the corner of the eye down over the cheek bone and past the mouth, but it was not very deep. I figured he might need a couple of stitches, but he might be lucky.

He pretty nearly sank his fingernails through my shoulder when I put the iodine on the cut, and again when I started poking the ugly looking bruises on his ribs.

"Jesus!" he cried out, but I clapped my hand over his mouth, his great hairy moustache tickling my skin, and nodded upwards to the ceiling to let him know that if he was not careful he'd have Ma down in no time flat and then there'd be one hell of a row.

"I'll be off, then," whispered Rory, leaning his big, red face close to us.

"All right, b'y," Daddy whispered back. "Thanks a million for your help."

"Think nothing of it. You can do the same for me some day."

From pushing and poking around I felt certain that none of Daddy's ribs was broken so I just smeared some kind of ointment on the affected area, ran a couple of bandages around him, and undressed him. When he had his nightshirt on,

I pointed upstairs to indicate I was going up to check on Ma. He nodded and grinned, holding up his glass in salute and taking a little drop of rum.

When I went up, put my ear to her door, I could plainly hear Ma snoring away quite happily. We were safe—at least until morning. -

"Right," I said as I came back down the stairs. "What the devil have you been up to this night, may I ask?"

"She all right?" he asked, rolling his eyes upwards.

"Snoring away like an old sow," I said.

"That's no way to be talking about your mother," he said sharply. "Have a little respect or I won't be telling you about today's adventure."

"Where were you? What happened? Was there a fight?"

"One at a time now, b'y, one at a time."

He took a gulp of rum and wiped his mouth on the back of his hand. "There's not a hell of a lot to tell, Donnie. This morning I went over to Waterford with

Angus MacEachern and while we were there the fellows got to talking about whether or not we could storm the power plant and get it back so the hospitals and all could be lit."

I nodded and urged him to continue. I knew that when the strike had been called the union had made an exception of the power plant at Waterford Lake which provided electricity to the town and surrounding areas, but that the company troops had seized it and cut off the power to homes and hospital alike.

"Well, we took her all right, sent the scabs home, and started her up again."

"Is that when you were hurt?"

"No, b'y, that was later. See, around nine o'clock or so the Goons came back. There was about a hundred of us fellows but there were more of them and they were armed to the teeth. They came galloping up and laid straight into us. Jesus, it was a real barney!"

"Was anyone else hurt, Daddy?"

"A few," he said with a grim nod, "but not many worse than me, I don't think. We were lucky."

"Well, you won't be lucky in the morning when Ma gets ahold of you," said I with a grin, "so you'd better be thinking up some kind of a story to tell her."

"It'll be the truth, Donnie," he said. "I know she'll blow her cork, but I never lied to her yet."

"I'll be listening for the screeching. Goodnight, Daddy."

"Goodnight, b'y," he said, pulling his nightshirt tighter around him.

Screeching there was too! Within minutes of my awakening the next morning I heard them at it below in the kitchen; Ma bawling and screaming, Daddy growling in reply.

I deliberately stayed in bed—something I have always hated doing once wide awake—until the noise had subsided. Finally, I heard the front door slam and Ma's footsteps going up the street. I pulled on my shirt and pants and hoofed downstairs.

"Jesus," I said as I came into the kitchen where Daddy, his face striped by a large plaster, was glowering in the rocking chair, "that was some donnybrook, by the sound of her!"

"Hmmph!" Daddy snorted. "And where the hell were you when I needed a little support?"

"Oh, no, not me, b'y. That was between you and the old woman!"

"She was fighting like a young she-wolf this morning," he said ruefully. "Oh my! My ears are burning and ringing from it all!"

"Well, it's over for a while. I heard her go up the street. Where was she heading?"

"Damned if I know, b'y. Away to your Aunt Sadie's place, I should imagine. I doubt we'll see her again afore nightfall."

"Oh, well, can't be helped, Daddy," I said, grabbing the teapot and hunting for a piece of bread. "What can't be cured must be endured."

"God! You're philosophical today, me son. Something like herself when she heats up a bit."

"Why, did she let drop another pearl of wisdom

today, then?"

"Not exactly a pearl," he said with a laugh, "and not too original, but possibly true. 'The older a man gets, the foolisher he gets,' she said, tossed her head and stalked out up the row."

I sniggered through a mouthful of the only piece of bread I could find, leathery and dry it was too, and snuffled up a few gulps of the bitter, black tea which had probably been stewing on the stove for a couple of hours.

I was just about to go hunting for something else to eat when there was a pounding on the door followed by big Lem Gillis stepping into the room.

"Morning, Mr. Ross. Morning, Donnie."

"Good day to you, Mr. Gillis," said my father. "What news brings you here so early of a morning?"

"Compliments of Mr. MacKay down the union office. A telephone call just come through from Waterford. Seems there was a terrible thing went on there this morning. The Goons run riot up Plummer Avenue, smashing windows and doors and beating up women and children. Mr. MacKay and Mr. Nearing said there's a meeting at nine and will you go along. There's room in the car they got."

"By Christ, I will!" Daddy exclaimed. "Tell Mr. MacKay I'll be ready when he calls. Donnie, you'll be coming, of course?"

"Try to keep me away."

"Sorry, Mr. Ross, Mr. MacKay said there's only one space in the automobile."

"That's all right, Daddy, I'll see if Little Jack will

take me over in his horse and trap."

"Right, then," Daddy said. "Off you go, Mr. Gillis."

Lem took off down the row while Daddy pulled on his big boots and I hopped over the fence to Little Jack's barn. He was puttering about inside, stacking bits and pieces of junk against the wall. I told him what I wanted.

"Jeez, Donnie, I'm willing to give it a try, but the poor old mare got a sharp stone in her foot a few days ago and I don't know if she'll stand it the whole way to Waterford."

"Give a try anyway, Jack," I urged, "the meeting's at nine. Get her hitched up and we'll take our chances."

Just as we were dragging the horse out of the barn, the loud spluttering of a motor-car came up the row. It was Alex MacKay and Joe Nearing come for Daddy. He squeezed in, boots shined, best hat on his head, and away they went roaring around the corner in a cloud of dust.

Jack and I climbed on the little trap and clattered after them. On the bend I saw Ma coming out of Aunt Sadie's front door, her arms waving aloft, her mouth open, a question plastered all over her shiny face.

"Faster, Jack!" I shouted, turning my head away so Ma would think I didn't see her. "Let's get out of here before she gets Heckie Milne's donkey."

"Oh, Jeez, the Angel of Death," he said, glancing over his shoulder at Ma's running figure. "I'd sooner drink lemonade for the rest of me life than run afoul of that tongue right now!"

Off we went, clopping through the dusty streets, the hooves echoing off the picket fences, the chickens squawking and fluttering out of the path, the washing lines defying the wind, the kids waving and jeering, the women shaking their heads and fists, the dogs chasing and yapping, the blue sky high, cool and indifferent to the acts of man.

Just past Dominion the mare started to limp and slowed down to a snail's pace; it was clear she was going no further.

"I was afraid of this," said Little Jack, shaking his head. "I guess I'll have to walk her home gentle. Goddamn it, it'll take me the best part of the day and I'll miss the fun."

"Sorry, Jack, it's my fault. I shouldn't have pressed you when the animal was none too well."

"Can't be helped, b'y," he said. "What'll you be doing now?"

"I'll hang around the highway to see if I can get a ride."

"All right, b'y, but don't forget to let me know all the details when yous get home tonight."

"It's a deal, Jack. Mind how you go."

I watched him hobble away back towards the little town, the dust almost obscuring him, then pulled a big stalk of grass and sat down on the bank for a chew.

All my life I have believed that early morning is the best time of day; the air is fresher, cleaner, the clouds not so tired, the colours crisper, brighter. Millions of people the world over have gone to the grave never knowing what it is like to roam abroad in the early light and cool sun; they may get up fairly early but they spend an hour fooling around in the house, then straight into the car or the bus to work without the chance to take stock of the day until noontime. It is their loss entirely.

Any road, this day, June 11, 1925, was a dandy, with the sun bright as new steel, turning the sea into a dazzle and streaking the undersides of the clouds with lemon gold. I couldn't see the Dump from the bank where I was sitting but to my right the Hub and Tablehead were in view, beyond them the Number Six District and further away still, appearing as a thin blue line, South Head. Away to my left was Lingan point and, below me, the long sand bar gently curving around to meet it. No boats out that morning, as I remember, but hundreds of gulls squawking and diving, screaming and circling in a mad, but brilliant display.

I took a good sniff of the salt air, stood up, dusted myself off, and set out along the road.

A little further along the highway, I noticed a cloud of dust on the Warburton Road and saw a buggy full of people charging down at breakneck speed. I buttoned my coat and sprinted to the junction and arrived there, panting for breath, just as the buggy reached the highway.

The driver was an O'Brien fellow I once worked with in the pit and he had a bunch of his neighbours with him.

"Good day!" he cried. "Danny Ross, isn't it?"

"Donnie," I corrected. "Mr. O'Brien, if I'm not mis-taken."

"Yessir, George is the name. Have you heard about the butchery that went on in Waterford a few hours ago?"

"Indeed I have and I was on my way there to go to the meeting."

"You'll not make it on foot, Donnie," he said, sneaking a look at his pocket-watch. "And unless I miss my guess it'll be getting under way pretty soon now."

"Can you squeeze me on somehow? My father is already gone by car."

"She's already filled to the brim, as you can see," he said with a backward motion of his head, "but if you can manage to hang on behind you're welcome to try."

"I'm obliged to you and I'll do my best."

Lord God! I wish I had stayed on that grassy bank gazing at the scenery, for there I was literally hanging on for grim death, no place to wedge my left foot and my arse about four inches from the ground.

The roads in those days were none too smooth and with each bump and pothole I thought the world was coming to an end. I was eating dust the whole time and my hands nearly dropped off from the pain, and the only relief I got was when we went through a puddle the other side of the bridge and my arse and legs were soaked to the skin.

Going up River Ryan Hill my right foot slipped out of its mooring and off I went, head over heels, into the ditch. By the time I had climbed out and shaken my head clear, the buggy was disappearing over the brow of the hill.

I had to go the rest of the distance on foot and that is why I missed the meeting at the school—but I did not miss the battle.

Just as I was wearily plodding down the slope into the town, I heard the noise first, then saw a gigantic column of people marching up the hill. There must have been four thousand of them and there was no mistaking they were out for blood for there was hardly a man who did not have a belt, stick, or rock in his hand.

As the host came nearer I searched the faces for those I knew. I didn't see Jim or Joe Nearing, though they must have been there, but I saw Alex MacKay and, close behind him, my father and Big Rory. Not far from them was a Mr. Muise I had met once or twice with his little dog scurrying by his side. Ahead of him was Angus MacEachern and Carl Haley, and away to the side Angus and Dougie MacDonald, looking like two dignified birds of prey, one of them an eagle, the other a hawk.

Tony Lucci was shambling along, a great ugly piece of iron in his mit and, near him, Barnabas Kelly, his blacksmith's apron tied up and full of big clinkers. Barry O'Toole and the Moose were striding purposefully along with a very military bearing.

There were even some women in the throng and, skipping about on the edges, a few children who had obviously disobeyed instructions to stay out of harm's way. I saw Gil Watson shouting at one of the kids to go home, but the little bugger just skeetered away only to re-emerge lower down the parade.

Some men were singing and one man, at least, was playing some kind of brass instrument for its vaguely martial braying came to me on the breeze.

Just as the head of the parade was drawing level with me I hopped down the bank and into the crowd to join Daddy, his head held high, his eyes staring into the distance and the plaster on his cheek making him look very grim. He looked sideways at me and raised an eyebrow.

"Took your time, didn't you?"

"If only you knew what troubles I've seen," I said, "you'd be right proud of me for being here at all today."

"Why, did you run afoul of the law?"

"I near ran afoul of Ma before I left, but that wasn't it. Little Jack's horse went lame, then I had to hang on the back of a buggy until I finally fell off the other side of River Ryan. I had to hoof it the rest of the way. I just got here."

"Well, I knew there had to be some kind of explanation for the way you look," he said, wrinkling up his nose. "You look like a low-class bum!"

I looked down at myself; he was right. The bottom half of me was still wet and caked with mud, the top half coloured a light brown with dust. My hands were raw and bleeding, my face felt scratched to hell, and my hair must have been like a hay stack in a hurricane.

"It's all in the cause," I said. "By the way, Da, what is it?"

"What's what?"

"The cause? Where are we going?"

"To Waterford Lake, b'y, to take back the power plant. We'll show those sons of whores this time. We got three thousand men at our back and they're all spoiling for a fight after what happened this morning."

"Did you find out what went on?"

"By God, yes. An act of terrorism it was, just like 'Bloody Sunday'. They came galloping down the main street with chains and whips and lashed out at everything and everybody in sight. The bastards even got off their horses and smashed into private homes, beating up the people!"

"Swine!"

"Aye, swine is right, b'y. They tell me an old crippled fellow got smashed up and some kids too,." His moustache twitched with indignation as he spoke. "I sure wouldn't want to be a company policeman this day, Donnie, I'll tell you that!"

After a while, the houses thinned out and the woods grew in close to the side of the road. I didn't know the area myself, but a fellow from Scotchtown who was marching on my left told me we were getting close to the lake.

We were approaching a bend in the road when a halt was called by the men up front and the host ground to a stop. Angus MacEachern shouted for quiet and then, after the talking had died down, we could hear it on the wind: the neighing of horses.

"Goons!" Daddy spat it out with contempt.

"Yes, sir, that's what it is all right, Tom," Alex MacKay said over his shoulder.

"What are we going to do?" a man shouted out.

"We don't know how many's there," Curly MacIsaac said. "Better be careful."

"We didn't come this far only to turn around and crawl back," Angus MacEachern cried. "Let's go get those sons of whores now!"

There was a great cheer from the crowd and, as one man, we pressed forward on round the bend. There they were, uniformed devils, revolvers in hand, astride great mounts with staring eyes and twitching ears. They were six abreast in the road and two or three up on the banks on either side, and they stretched back all the way to the yard of the power plant. All I could see was Goons, horses, and guns, and my blood ran cold.

"Jesus Christ! There must be a couple of hundred of them!"

"But there's a couple of thousand of us, b'y," said Daddy.

"But they've got guns, for Christ's sake. What have we got?" As I asked the question I looked at my own hands and realized they were empty of any weapon. My belly contracted with fear as I desperately wondered what to do.

The decision was made for all of us. One of the troopers levelled his revolver and fired into the crowd, at which sign they dug their heels into their mounts and galloped forward, shooting as they came.

"Into the woods!" I heard myself screaming, and as I scrambled over the ditch, I noticed that others had the same idea.

A bullet whined past my ear and embedded itself into a tree stump ahead of me. As I looked round I saw a huge black horse coming straight at me and I hurled myself back into the ditch, letting out a yell as one of the hind hooves caught my left arm, making it go numb from top to bottom.

I scrambled to my feet the best I could and, grabbing an old fence post, laid about me with a will. I got a glimpse of Daddy across the road lashing a Goon with his belt and another of Tony Lucci swinging the iron bar over his head.

All around the horses were panicking; whinnying, and rearing up, ofttimes throwing their riders to the ground where the men pounded upon them with stick and boot.

I saw a Goon raising his revolver to shoot a fellow and I let him have it across the back with the fence post. He screamed, dropped the gun, and wheeled around to face me, drawing a great riot stick from its sheath. He lurched forward and pounded the life out of my right shoulder and neck before being hauled from his saddle by two big miners and stomped into the dirt.

Now I couldn't use either one of my arms so, considering myself worse than useless for fighting, I staggered into the woods and wedged myself down behind a couple of bushes.

No sooner than I was settled to nurse my wounds than an injured Goon came stumbling past within a few feet of me. I stuck out my foot and brought him down, then swung round and sent my other boot smashing into his face. He groaned and rolled over, out to the world.

Looking back to the road I could see that the battle was ours. By scattering into the woods, the men had lured the Goons into riding deeper and deeper into the throng of marchers and, when they had passed, closed back in behind them. Surrounded, the Goons lost their flexibility and the horses went berserk. I saw one big bay go charging past, dragging a Goon face downward, his foot trapped and twisted in the stirrup.

Beyond the ditch on the other side I saw an O'Handley fellow fall and a big grey horse run right over the top of him. Denny Morrison was struggling with a Goon and when he grabbed the pistol had half his hand blown off.

The shots, the curses, the clanging and clattering of the battle filled the air; the sky was almost black with clinker and stones as they hurtled down on the Goons like rain; the dust flew in great clouds, and the woods were alive with the crashing of the fugitives as they tried to escape.

Mr. Muise's little dog came scurrying over to me, whimpering with fear and pain, and nuzzled himself up against me. Its face was streaming with blood and when I took a good look the reason was clear: a bullet had taken the poor animal's nose clean off.

The battle lasted no more than ten or fifteen minutes from beginning to end. The Goons were completely routed; some had galloped away, dozens had plunged into the woods, the rest were rounded up and placed under arrest. I clambered out of my hiding place and onto the road to join Daddy and the others who were surveying the shambles.

There were five bodies lying in the road, all of them miners. Two were unconscious but were breathing well and appeared not to have any serious damage. The O'Handley man was in terrible shape, shot and trampled by the horses' hooves, a mass of mangle and blood with scarcely a breath in his body.

Another body turned out to be Gil Watson, whom I had earlier seen shouting at one of the boys, whose hands were clutched to a gore-soaked stomach, and who looked like he didn't have long to wait for the end.

"Here's another fellow," shouted Angus from the side. "Looks like he's fainted."

"Probably out from a sock on the head," said Alex. "Get some water, we'll probably be able to bring him around."

"Look," Daddy said, pulling aside the man's coat and pointing to a neat, red-edged hole just over the heart, "this fellow's dead as dog meat."

"Who is he?"

"No idea, b'y."

"Ask around, see if any of the men know him. I imagine he's got a family."

The men crowded around, peering down at the dead man's face. There was a great murmuring as men suggested identities and were contradicted by others.

Finally a man poked his head over the shoulders of the crowd, took a look, and pushed forward.

"I know him," he said to Angus. "He's a Davis fellow. I worked with him in Twelve pit."

And so it turned out to be. William Davis, militant hero according to some, the original innocent bystander to others, he gave his life and his name to the miners' memorial day, which we have celebrated on that date ever since.

Nobody knows who shot him or what he was doing there. He was never noted as an active union man and, according to one of his daughters, he had gone out that day to buy a nipple for the baby's bottle. Maybe he couldn't resist a parade and for yielding to the temptation to join the march was murdered by the BESCO police.

Amazingly, I learned later, Watson and Mickey O'Handley recovered and lived on for a number of years after.

Seizing the power plant was child's play once the Goons had been thrashed. The scabs inside burst their way through the back of the plant and struck out into the forest. In the retelling of the story afterwards, the scabs moved so fast and were so filled with fear of the mob that they ran across Waterford Lake on the surface of the water!

Suffice it to say they were chased to hell out and

the plant was smashed up, something our leaders had not wanted, but were powerless to prevent, so great was the rage of the people.

Not satisfied with wrecking the plant they fanned out into the woods and rounded up the fugitives, bringing them back to the yard, bleeding and trembling, and then frog-marched them into town, beating and abusing them the whole way.

When we stopped to rest, one of the captured Goons turned to another fellow prisoner, calling him "Captain."

Tommy Ling whirled around, as did Angus and my father, their ears cocked, their eyes wide. The man flinched visibly and drew himself erect as they moved in on him.

"What's your name, scum?" Angus demanded.

"MacDonald," he said defiantly. "Andrew MacDonald from Halifax."

"What's your rank?"

"Sergeant," he said, knowing we could not tell from the few tatters hanging from his back.

"Well, I guess you don't mind if we search you, Sergeant MacDonald," said Tommy, running his hands over the man's remaining pockets. They were empty.

As they stood there, glaring at each other, a youngster came running up, holding out what looked like a blue card.

"I found this back apiece in the ditch," said the boy, handing it to Angus.

He took it from the boy. It was a bank book and

when opened it showed a balance of $1,743 and was in the name of D.A. Noble.

Angus went white, and he turned back to the prisoner. "Does this belong to you, Goon?"

"No," replied the man, his chin held up, his eyes blazing back. "I never saw it before in my life."

"Are you Noble?" Angus screamed in his face, grabbing the man by the neck, digging his fingers deep into the flesh.

"Andrew MacDonald," came the throttled reply.

Angus backed off, looked around at the other men, spat in the prisoner's face, and made a motion for the column to move on.

To this day, we do not know if we had Noble in our grasp that day and I think it was best we had no proof, for had we been sure the man would certainly have been murdered on the spot.

The Goons, once marched into town, were locked up in the jail and Daddy and I headed back across country to make the peace with Ma.

As the story of the Battle of Waterford Lake spread throughout the coalfields it took on an almost religious significance, its deeds exaggerated, its horrors multiplied, its heroism magnified, and with all this Billy Davis's reputation grew by leaps and bounds. He had been leading the march, some said, holding a banner aloft in defiance and singing the "Red Flag." Others had him fighting three policemen with his bare hands when they gunned him down. One story had him defending the honour of a widow woman who was bravely resisting the lewd advances of a drunken Goon.

The skeptics, like Adam Francis, said it was just a stray bullet and Billy happened to be in its path.

In any event, as the story was told and retold on street corners, in back kitchens, in union halls, the anger of the people grew to the boiling point. Revenge was demanded, reprisals planned. Indeed, Daddy and I learned that after we had left New Waterford that day there had been a crowd of men who had wanted to set fire to the jail with the company Goons inside, and it took a great deal of persuasion to talk them out of it.

Nor was that the end, for later still, we were told, the Goons were released from the jail and taken to the railroad station where they were put on a train to Sydney. When the news leaked out the men went wild and stormed the station with bars and ropes, ready to wreck the station and hang the Goons. Angus, who told us about it, said an outrage was only avoided by the local clergymen and priests linking arms and barring the way.

The mood of the men was ugly and at Bill Davis's funeral you could feel it in the air and hear it muttering on the breeze. Over four thousand people followed Davis's casket to the cemetery and pretty near every one of them was set on vengeance of some kind.

Daddy and I went over, of course, and every person we spoke to was breathing trouble. Tommy Ling was particularly wound up and, apparently, didn't mind who heard his opinions, be they miner, priest, or policeman. Later we learned that Tommy was arrested that night and was only let out of jail by a vote of the town council, which also fired the cops who arrested him! Needless to say, the Labour Party controlled the council.

It was clear to anyone with the sense of a flea that something had to break, and that night the fires started.

The first one was in New Waterford—Bill Davis's home town—when just after night had fallen the Number Twelve Colliery wash-house went up in a sheet of flame. The following night the company store at Caledonia was attacked, robbed, and burned to the ground, the word being that $50,000 worth of stuff had been taken.

Daddy was shaken: he did not know whether to applaud or condemn the burnings.

"Don't misunderstand me, Donnie," he said, as we sat around the kitchen table two nights later, "I loathe to see anything that man has built with his hands destroyed, but it is no wonder that the people want to drive the company from this place—by fire or sword!"

"Well, they are certainly using the fire," I said.

"There's some that say the company set the fire themselves to discredit the union," said Dinny Murphy, who was in for a wet of tea, "but it's hard to think the company would take that kind of action."

"You never know, Dinny, you never know," my father said. "The company is being run by some of the blackest swine that ever drew breath and I wouldn't put anything past the likes of that."

"Daddy, you may as well face the fact," I said. "I was talking to at least three fellows today who were boasting of the stuff they had lifted from the Caledonia store—shoes and grub and stuff like that."

"Well, if it's true, then all I can say is that the stuff was needed. God knows there's enough starving children and barefooted youngsters about here these days."

"I wonder if it isn't a bad tactic," I ventured carefully. "It seems to me it's the last thing we need right now."

"How so, Donnie?" Dinny asked.

"You didn't hear? I just got the news coming in a half hour ago. The place is crawling with troops. There's five hundred just come in from Halifax, a bunch of new Goons from Halifax harbour, and a big squad on its way from some place in Ontario."

"By the Jesus!" Daddy exclaimed. "Why didn't you tell me?"

"I never got the chance. I only just sat down when you and Dinny here were yakking away nineteen to the dozen."

"Five hundred, you say, and more on the way?"

"That's the word down the union hall," I said. "That's what I'm talking about, see? You start burning and the next thing you know your brains are smashed out by soldiers and your family is mowed down by a machine-gun."

"But a man just can't sit quietly by and take it." Daddy was getting heated, his eyes flashing. "Just as well to roll over and die like an old mule. I tell you, you can't stop people from rising against injustice. Look what happened in Russia. Now maybe a lot of it didn't make sense and maybe some buildings got burned, but the people had to be heard, they had to be victorious."

"Well, neither one of us has been there, with all due respect, Daddy, and Jesus only knows what's really going on over there. For all we know the work- ers are still getting shot."

I thought Daddy was going to have a heart attack, he was that choked up over what I had said, his eyes bulging, his colour reddening, his breathing getting heavy. He shook his head and blew a great, vibrating breath through his moustache.

"God protect me," he said. "I thought I had enough with its mother, but this is really trying my patience. Is it sucked in by the capitalist press you are, Don- nie? Is that it? Is it after reading the *Sydney Post* that you've come to these brilliant conclusions? Maybe its a job with Mr. Wolvin you want. Private secretary or something! Jesus, Dinny, get him from here before I strike him!"

"Take it easy, Tom," said Dinny, looking worried. "Here, have another cup of tea. It's still hot."

Any further argument was spared by a thumping at the door and Little Jack's head poking around it. He was red in the face and out of breath.

"Come quick, Tom! The company store's afire!"

"What? Which one?"

"Every Jesus one in the world as far as I can figure," panted Little Jack. "Come in the street. You can see ours at the top of the row. She's roaring away like timber!"

"Holy Christopher!" Dinny yelled, knocking the cup onto the floor as he jumped to his feet. "Let's get going!"

As soon as we got outside the door we were aware of it. The night was red and bright from the flames and at the top of the row we could see the fire leaping skyward from a building which would never open its doors again. Everywhere people were scurrying from their houses and making for the scene, their faces bright and eerie from the glare.

Old Mother Williams, touched in the head, clung to the little tree by her front gate, her eyes shining, a silly grin on her face. "It's the end of the world, Tom Ross!" she shouted as we passed by. "The Lord is sending fire upon the firmament to make the sinners perish for their misdeeds."

"That's right," I called back. "You'd better get ready, for the Second Coming is at midnight!"

"Don't be tormenting the poor soul," Daddy snapped at me. "As if there wasn't enough misery about without the likes of you trying to make it worse."

When we reached the store there was very little of it left and, as we pushed our way through to the front of the gathering crowd, we felt the heat on our faces and were almost deafened by the roar and crackle of the flames as they shot into the blackness above. The one remaining section of the building, a teetering dark patch in the brightness, suddenly keeled over and crashed to the ground where it was consumed by a great burst of fire which threw sparks and cinders in all directions, sending the crowd scattering backwards.

"This is a strange night's work," said Dinny as we walked back.

"It is indeed," Daddy replied. "But whose work is it? I don't see anyone running around with stolen goods."

"If the store had been looted, they would have been long gone before we came," I said.

"There speaks the agent of the company again!" Daddy barked, giving me a baleful glare. "Always looking for the worst possible interpretation he is, Dinny."

"I only want you to be able to face the truth, whatever it turns out to be," I said.

"The truth is something we may never know," Dinny intoned profoundly. "Come morning we'll be hearing a hundred stories about tonight, and all of them different."

"Tom! Donnie!" Eldrid MacIntyre called to us from up by the church. "Come up on the tump. The whole world's ablaze!"

We rushed over to him and followed him up the hill. Halfway up I chanced to glance down at the colliery; the light from the fire made it easy to see what was going on.

I grabbed Daddy's arm and pointed to the helmeted figures. "There! See them? Troops. Laying barbed wire around her, they are."

"I see the devils," he said. "Are they trying to keep us out, or what?"

"Guess they're afraid we'll set the mine on fire, too," ventured Eldrid, his little, round face bobbing up and down as he spoke.

"What's going on over the gate?" Dinny asked, pulling me to him and making me look along his arm.

There was a group of soldiers assembling some kind of equipment, the clanking of the metal just audible and the light flashing from it.

"Jesus!" Daddy exclaimed as he peered down. "I've seen the likes of that before. It's a machine-gun. They must be setting up a nest right here in the Dump."

"We'd best be careful what we're about in the neighbourhood now," said Dinny. "I don't fancy me arms and legs scattered from here to the Glory Hole!"

"Amazing what they can do to a man, them things," said Eldrid. "I seen them at work in the war when I was in France. Two fellows could hold off fifty or more with one of them guns. One fellow to aim and the other fellow to feed the cartridges in. The only problem is they gets stuck when they've been firing a lot. The heat, I think."

"Thank you, Eldrid, for your remarkable technical dissertation," Daddy said dryly. "Now what in the name of time are we coming up here for anyhow?"

"Come up here and stand on the big rock."

We struggled to the top of the tump and clambered up onto the rock. The whole sky was cast in orange and pink. To our left, in Glace Bay, two great fires blazed into the night, one at New Aberdeen and the other further away. Beyond that, we could see a red glow from the Number Six District and, straight ahead of us, two more at Reserve. Away to our right hand, Dominion was marked by a soft, deep-red splurge of light, like an opening flower.

"Christ! It is the end of the world!" Dinny cried.

"The revolution, more like," growled Daddy. "I never saw anything like it in my whole life."

"What's the fire beyond Number Two?" I asked.

"Must be Caledonia," said Eldrid. "It's about the right position."

"Can't be Caledonia," said Dinny with a nervous laugh, "that was already burned down two days ago. They can't be burning down something was already burned."

"It must be Number Eleven," said Daddy. "My God, what a night!"

"Why the two fires in Reserve, Tom?" Dinny asked, clutching his sleeve and pointing them out. "There's only the one store there."

"Blessed if I know, b'y, but there's not likely a pluckme standing in the whole place."

"Yeah, Tom, a fellow back there told me the Sydney Mines store was destroyed yesterday, too."

"Holy Christopher," Dinny muttered to himself, "what a night. What a night!"

We stood there, in awe of men's deeds, and overwhelmed by the size of the inky night and of the flaming eruptions that painted themselves onto the sky. It was a night neither we nor anyone else in Cape Breton would ever forget.

13: That leaden sky

I was as fretful as a colt all of the next week, waiting for the weekend to come, to see Jeanette again! I paid scant attention to my union business and was nothing but a pain in the arse around the house.

I don't know why I had said two weeks when I could just as easily have gone back to the farm after only one, but when people go away from home they think the whole place is falling apart without them and that they'll need a long time to straighten things out again. They always go back home too soon and, when they get there and find out hardly anybody knew they were gone, immediately wish they'd never left.

"Lord love you," said Ma, exasperated with my mooning about the place, "you're clucking around my kitchen like an old red hen with eggs that won't hatch. What in the name of time has gotten into you?"

"Ah, I'm just getting restless with the strike, Ma. I'll be off to Poppy's on Friday. A breath of fresh air will do me good."

"Sounds to me like it's more than a bit of fresh air that's dragging you back there so soon, Donnie," said

Daddy, peering over the top of the paper. "Had to browbeat you to get you there once a year till now, and now you're gallivanting off there every five minutes."

"Yes, and it's a deal more than fresh air will be needed to get the stench of this God-forsaken strike out your system," Ma snapped, rescuing me from Daddy's probing. "If a body had any sense they'd move out to the country permanent. Grow a few vegetables and make themselves useful to God and man instead of rotting around here trying to best the proper authorities and set fires and such like."

"It's like a parrot, that's what it is," Daddy muttered as he threw the crumpled paper on the settle and stomped out into the yard.

And on Friday I was off. The wind and the spring in my heels, it seems I flew the whole distance—in my mind that is, for it took a hefty chunk of day by horse and cart—and I arrived a little after nightfall. I went to the little white room and fell asleep on the featherbed dreaming of love.

How I cursed that leaden sky when I awoke that Saturday morning. I pleaded and begged the sun to come out, as if the grey weather would somehow spoil our reunion.

Then I thought: hadn't we made love in grey weather, had not we stood naked in the rain, laughing at the dark clouds and then, clutching our unnecessary clothing under our arms, run wet and gleaming towards the shelter of the forest?

Heartened, I pulled on a raincoat and set out

through the damp, heavy-smelling woods. Our little bank was glistening with raindrops and I sat down and pulled my coat around me.

I waited until nightfall, but she did not come. A grown man, I sat, soaking wet, on a misty patch of grass in the middle of nowhere, sobbing helplessly, crying like a baby. My eyes were raw-red when I got back to the farm and all night long I muffled my moans of pain in the pillow.

Neither the next day, nor the next week, nor any other week did I find her at the appointed meeting place. I searched all the other farms in the area in the hope that she had been confused in the arrangement. I even stood alone in my misery, in the heart of the dripping woods or out in the grey drizzle of a field, calling, shouting, screaming her name. I made enquiries around the neighbourhood to see if anyone had seen or heard of anyone answering to her description, but all I got were shaking heads and puzzled glances.

After a few weeks of this torture, I finally realized that she knew who I was and where I could be reached and that if she had not already done so, it could only mean that she did not want to find me. For summers after, however, I would return to that bank, half hoping to see her, but not surprised when I did not.

That's over fifty years ago, yet still those memories are fresh and full of pain.

When I was almost sixty, my son took me for a drive around that same countryside where I had known such joy. It had changed, of course, but the place was still peaceful. Poppy's old farm was bleached and bare but in the yard was a blue Cadillac with New York licence plates. Not far away, a few yards from the roadside, I saw a tiny cemetery and as we passed I glimpsed the name MacLellan carved on a large marble headstone.

I shouted to my son to stop the car, scrambled out, and ran to the spot.

MacLELLAN

HERE LIE THE REMAINS OF JEANETTE ANNE
BELOVED WIFE OF RICHARD
BORN OCTOBER 1882, DIED JULY 1945
MAY SHE REST IN PEACE

I ran my hands over the cold stone, my mind racing. Eighteen eighty-two, I thought, that would have made her forty-three when we met.

It was impossible. I had chased another rainbow and found nothing. It was a very common name, I told myself on the way home in the car, and the tears ran down my old cheeks and down under my collar.

So I dragged myself home again. The strike was still smouldering, its very smell on the air.

As I approached the row's children came running up to me, asking me did I know that so-and-so was in hospital or that this child or that had died, and I would nod affirmatively because it was impossible to converse with them, they were so noisy and all spoke at the same time. Their parents were less vocal and most simply nodded as I strode past. Men that I knew well would wave or leave the step where they were sitting and come over to me. At each such step their conversation was almost identical.

"How did you get on in the country?"

"Good. How's she going yourself?"

"She's bad, Donnie, b'y, the worst I ever seen."

"Any breaks yet?"

"Don't look like it."

"Pretty bad, eh?"

"Yes, she's bad all right."

"Well, see you."

"Yeah, see you, Donnie."

Crooked Billy had the worst news for me as I turned the corner onto our street. When he saw me he heaved himself off the step, through the gate, and came hobbling up the row, his crutches flying in the dust.

"Your Dad is in jail," he said without any formalities.

"In jail?" This was bad news indeed. "What for?"

"Inciting a riot, down by the Town Hall. Day before yesterday. Him and Rannie Corbett. They grabbed them for saying the place should be burned down."

"Daddy?" I cried. "That doesn't sound like him. He's never done anything like that before."

"Nor he didn't this time neither," said Billy, spitting on the ground. "Rannie was calling for the burning and your Dad was trying to tell them no."

"Then why for Christ's sake did they jail him?"

"They was both up there on the steps ashouting and speechmaking, so I guess they just grabbed the both of them and locked 'em up."

"How's Ma?"

"Your Ma is all right," he said, rubbing his bristled chin with the top of his crutch. "She's used to this stuff b'now."

"That's true, I guess, but it doesn't make things easier."

"How'd she go in the country?" he asked.

"All right," I said, lying to myself and to Billy.

"And your good grandfolk?"

"Hale and hearty."

"Good people they are," he spat again. "Knew them personally myself."

"I'd better go see Ma. See you around, Billy."

Ma was in the kitchen, sitting in the old rocker darning socks. Her face was thin and drawn and she barely looked up when I went in.

"You're back," she said flatly.

"Good to see you, Ma," I said, going up to her and brushing my lips against her cheek.

"You heard about your father, did you?"

"Yes, Billy told me in the street."

"Disgracing us in front of the whole town," she said bitterly. "I should never have married him. I should never have left the country."

"Ma! How could you?" I was horrified to find her like this, so cold and bitter. "Daddy's a fine man and you know it."

"Do I?" She turned her cool eyes on me. "Do I know that, Donnie? All I know is that ever since I came to this God-forsaken town we have known nothing but strife and trouble and your father's the cause of it. Him and his ideas!"

"Those ideas, as you call them, are things men died for. We call them principles." I was hard and cold.

"You don't find country people always scrapping for more, always grumbling about this and that, calling down the government and the church. It's a disgrace and an abomination to the Lord!"

"You're upset," I said, not wanting to be drawn into a political argument. "You don't know what you're saying."

"I know what I'm saying, all right," she flared, her eyes burning. "And that's another thing. Disrespect for your own mother! What next will it be? Adultery no doubt."

She attacked the sewing, yanking at the thread with her teeth. "Our reward is in heaven, I say, not here on earth. The Bible says so, but you and him won't believe the Bible. Oh, no, not you. Not the smart socialists who know everything!"

"Ma—" I made to interrupt, but she turned again, her tongue biting into my soul.

"I say again, Donald, if we were meant to have short hours and high pay, God would have given it to us."

"That's nonsense!" I cried angrily.

"Nonsense? Insult your own mother, go ahead,

that's all you free-thinkers are good for. Destroy what's holy and bite the hand that feeds you."

"My God, Ma," I said, "you're saying all the things the officials say."

"Quite right, too," she said defiantly. "They know more than you do. They're all educated men and why shouldn't they know what's best?"

"Because they're liars and thieves," I shouted, completely losing my temper, "and I never expected to find a scab in my own home!"

"What?" She looked up, her face turning stony.

"Nothing," I mumbled and turned away towards the sink.

"Nothing was it? Well, let me tell you this, Donald Ross, your father is in jail for breaking the law. It's no more than he deserves. But you..." she shook her head rapidly, "you will hang because you're worse than he is!"

I went in next door to Black Jim's house and scrounged a bit to eat. It was only tea and bread but it was good and it took my mind off the fight I had just had with Ma.

Here the people seemed cheerful enough, scratching by on scraps, potatoes, and hope. I have no idea how, but Black Jim was as fat and hearty as ever and seemed to complain little about the meagre fare he was being served and old Peglegs seemed to be enjoying every minute of the strike sitting in the corner in his rocking chair, chuckling to himself with each new event whether good or, as in most cases, bad.

"Heh, heh, Donnie, b'y, you got to get 'em on both

knees before they'll see any sense. One knee ain't enough. Starve 'em I say, starve 'em good and maybe then they'll see the system for what it really is."

Somewhat cheered by the scant but friendly meal, I set off into town to report at the union hall. It was an old, warped building not far from the colliery known simply as Dump Hall.

Some of the meeting places in the area acquired grand and glorious names, such as The Barrel of Blood, where the Communist Party used to gather and where my father often held forth on the theory of surplus value or on the inevitability of world-wide revolution. I was never a communist myself although I was often branded as such, usually by people who did not know what communism was and would not know a communist if they fell over one in the street.

It was a useful label to pin on anyone who stood up for his rights and up until this day, some people are still using that tactic, hoping that religious or ignorant folk will be scared out of their wits. It often worked for them and then, for good measure, they threw in atheist, bigamist and a thousand other names designed to stir the prejudice of their audience. So fine, honest, and truly God-fearing men were scandalized and ruined in this fashion long before Senator McCarthy discovered that insecure people could be incited to fever pitch by the mere mention of a few words.

The next morning I left the house early and went to the Town Hall to see if I could get Dad out of jail. Ma was still in an ornery mood, barely speaking as she served me a scant breakfast of fried potatoes and tea, and I guessed that the only way to calm her down was to restore my father to the household to remove, in effect, the "disgrace" which he had supposedly brought upon us.

Try as I would, I could not convince my mother that to be jailed during a strike was something approaching an honour and by no means a disgrace, but she steadfastly held to her country beliefs that man was born ignorant and should not try to better his lot unless so blessed by a noble birth.

Frank Regan was desk sergeant for the day, but was not very helpful. Bail had been granted but had been set at fifty dollars, a sum the magistrate, Frank's cousin, must have known was far beyond the reach of a striking miner.

I had always found Frank a likeable sort of man for a policeman, but today vent all my frustrations on him for his cousin's actions. I could appreciate why townspeople had little use for the Regan family for, as the legend went, a man would ride to town on a tram driven by Paddy Regan, get drunk in Joe Regan's tavern, be arrested by Frank Regan and eventually be tried by Hector Regan.

I related this to him in my best bar room manner, but at his threat to lock me up with Daddy, I beat a hasty retreat into the street, where I bumped into Fiddler on his way to the Dump Hall.

"Good day, Donnie, b'y. Going up the hall?"

"No, Fiddler," I replied, "I think I'll go for a walk to try and sort things out."

"Mind if I go along?" he asked, and then added, "I have a tiny drop of rum I won from a Sydney man at cards last night."

"Why not?" I was indifferent.

"I don't know how pure it is," said Fiddler dubiously, "but it smells like rum and tastes like rum."

"What the hell!"

"What's wrong, b'y?" Fiddler asked, putting his arm around my shoulders and propelling me towards the beach.

"The whole Jesus mess, Fiddler, I'm sick of it. And now I can't even get Daddy out of the clink."

"Bail?"

"Fifty bucks!"

"Jesus, Mary, and Joseph," he whistled, "they don't mean for him to get out, do they?"

"He wasn't even tried yet," I said angrily.

"Pooh, what's that? A trial? My dear man, he was tried and convicted the minute they laid hands on him."

Fiddler stopped and looked at me. "They can't let troublemakers run around loose. Use your head, now. My God, b'y, if they were to free all the men who went around criticizing them, the country would be brought to its knees." His voice assumed a pompous tone and he waved his hands in the air. "The economy would collapse, the system would crumble!"

"You really believe that horseshit?"

"No," he said solemnly, "I don't. In fact, I believe the opposite is true. The more stunts they pull like this, the more chance there is of their power being taken from them. People will only tolerate so much repression for so long until a point is reached when they rise up and say, 'Enough!'"

"Maybe Peglegs is right," I said.

"What does he say?"

"He says that you have to starve the workers before they'll wake up, put them down on two knees. He says one knee isn't enough."

"There's something in that," Fiddler admitted, "but it's more complicated than that. I pretend to understand, Donnie, but I'm not sure I do."

We wandered down to the little field where Hoppy MacKinnon kept his animals and hoisted ourselves up on the old fence. Hoppy's horses were at the far end of the rough pasture, looking lean and sad. The old cow, little more than a bag of bones, plodded towards us, pushing her nose around the backs of our coats.

"Even they are suffering because of the strike," I said with a sigh.

"Sure," Fiddler rejoined, "especially them. They're the first to suffer and it's a marvel to me that Hoppy didn't kill the works of them to eat."

"A good horsesteak would go down pretty well right now," I said with a grin.

"With strong beer, roast potatoes, new greens, gravy and," his eyes twinkled, "a quart of good rum for after."

"Surely, you're not thinking of—"

"God, no! I wouldn't do a thing like that, not to an old friend like Hoppy. Still..."

"For the love of Christ, let's go," I said quickly, "before we're tempted to drag one behind the barn and eat it raw."

"What's going to happen, Fiddler?" I asked as we strolled on down the row.

"When, now or after?"

"After. Years from now. Will we ever see it?"

"I don't think," he said sadly, "but our children might. And that's worth fighting for. To be sure, they'll get more sly. They'll phase out these rough methods, but they'll always be the same. What you'll probably see is the church dropping this opposition to unions and see them nosing their way in and taking them over, making sure that all good, moderate Catholics are elected to the top positions. Then the governments will set up labour-company boards to contaminate the union leaders with easy living and blind them with reason. And, my friend, when that happens, men like you and me will have a double fight. We'll be fighting the company and our own leaders."

"You make it sound pretty bad, Fiddler. Do you really think it will ever be like that?"

"Mark my words, b'y, it's coming. Things will be better that way-a little bit, anyway. The first signs will be when we start paying our leaders as much as the company pays theirs."

"Where'd we get that kind of money?"

"When you get bigger unions and higher dues."

"What about strikes?" I asked with a laugh. "One good strike would wipe out the funds. Look at us now, for God's sake, only a few lousy thousand dollars from the International."

"The International!" Fiddler repeated it with obvious distaste. "That's another thing we'll regret—Leaving people in another country tell us what to do."

"Well, a few thousand is better than nothing."

"Maybe," he said thoughtfully. "Maybe."

I dismissed most of what he said as idle speculation, not guessing how prophetic time would prove him. The irony of it was, however, that when that foreseen day did arrive Fiddler was one of the first to fall for the bait.

Years later, when I reminded him of those words, he claimed not to remember and urged me to stop dreaming and "keep up with the times." But that was very much later and, at the time, Fiddler was one of the most outstanding unionists we had, exemplary and incorruptible, a tower of strength in the local and a good man to have around at any time.

The strike dragged on and times became harsher. Infant deaths were more frequent and people took on an almost ghostly appearance. I was too bound up with my own problems to give union matters my proper attention and weekends I still rushed out to the country chasing my elusive dreams. Ma softened a little and we got back on speaking terms more.

Inevitably, we crumbled and gave in when the government appointed a Royal Commission to investigate the strike and its causes and to recommend what should be done. Sir Andrew Rae Duncan and his starchy colleagues, fresh, I suspected, from the stock exchanges of London and Toronto, recommended wage cuts, bad enough, but not as severe as the company had initially tried to enforce.

Daddy was let out of jail and no more was heard of his case. The men trickled back to work, but several collieries had been closed down forever, leaving hundreds without jobs.

As soon as I heard this I knew we had been duped. We had played right into their hands, for it was now obvious that they had been determined to cut coal production, and they used the strike as an excuse not to reopen the mines. That some of those closed pits were the most militant in the district was no accident and I wept at our foolishness.

Edgar Rhodes won his election and became premier and John Willie MacLeod retired shortly afterwards.

Hilbert MacVarish used to tell me that no strike was ever really lost because it taught you valuable lessons about life. By Hilbert's standards we won the 1925 strike hands down because it taught us lessons aplenty and brought out the very best and very worst in our people. The creeping midnight stealth of the Judas, carrying names and details to the company with an ingratiating leer, was more than offset by the generosity of those who gave to others while leaving themselves short, and by the strange good humour which our adversity generated.

I remember the laughs over the wholesale swapping of boots following the ransacking of the company stores, with fellows asking in at houses if they could exchange a left foot for a right foot. I remember the good spirits among the neighbours when we smelled something good cooking in one of the houses and asked if had seen the cat lately. Anyone

For all I know maybe some people did toss the odd cat into the pot, for there was little else to cook, but it is easy to get things out of focus when you are looking back over fifty years or more and I often wonder just how much of our legend has basis in fact.

I have listened to four different versions of certain events from fellows who were all eyewitnesses to them and none of them agreed with what I remembered. We have got so many salty talkers around here that, with each telling of the tale, the more dramatic among us will colour and embellish the story as we go along.

I was listening to an old fellow on the radio the other day—know him well and used to work with him in the pit—and he was calling those of us who were active in 1925 "working class heroes." He is entitled to his moments of glory, I guess, but I certainly cannot recall having felt like a hero at the time.

They were hard and rough and stirring times all right and a lot of people suffered to an extent that should never again be allowed, but I do not feel we considered ourselves heroic figures acting out life's drama on the social battleground.

We did what had to be done. We did what we thought was right and some of us took a real beating;

some of us lost our lives.

The old fellow was saying on the radio, "We stood shoulder to shoulder and stared down the gun barrels at the denizens of evil." That fellow can really spin a yarn.

The problem, as I recall it, was that the situation was less like the frontline of a battlefield and more like the back streets of a city under siege. The frustration and helplessness arose from the fact it was not, apart from the Waterford incident, a pitched battle where we could see the whites of their eyes, but a war of nerves in which the enemy fought through the pages of the newspapers and we defended the ramparts by talking amongst ourselves and trying to keep up the spirits of the young, bewildered and excited, and the old, cornered and uncomprehending.

The 1925 strike was like what somebody once said about God: if it had not taken place it would have been necessary for Cape Breton to have invented it.

14: Comrade Jim

No sooner were we catching our breath a bit than the thirties were upon us and the people of the Prairies and the big Ontario cities got a taste of what we had been through so many times. We'd had plenty of idle times around here up to that point and we were in for lots more of them during the next decade or so. In fact,

I don't think unemployment has ever been lower than ten per cent in this area, so it is something we're used to. Used to, yes, but, by Jesus, we still don't like it and we never will.

So the thirties were hard times for us, just as the twenties were hard times for us, and life went on. Marg and I got married and Ruby was born.

Towards the end of the decade we left the old house and moved down here; same kind of house, same district, just a matter of yards. The men still grumbled with good reason, the boys still played ball in back over there, the girls still looked good in summertime. Ma and Daddy grew a little older, a little greyer, and Dorothy Dix was still pushing advice to the lovelorn and the brokenhearted.

Ma kept on taking Dr. Chase's liver pills and every

time I opened the paper little Jack Daw was running around in the sun. Once in a blue moon the little ones would get a bar of Fry's Extra Cream and if it gave them constipation someone would ram Cartoria mixture down their throats.

The union was still going strong and so, of course, was Jim MacLachlan.

In 1931, just after he turned sixty, the locals clubbed together and sent him on a trip to Russia for several months, where he even got as far as Siberia. He came back with glowing reports but with nagging misgivings about Stalin and the beginnings of what he thought were harmful trends.

No sooner had he returned from the Soviet Union, however, than he was locking horns with the Communist Party, whose line was that the miners should stay with Lewis and the U.M.W. when Jim was trying to persuade them to break away and bring back the old Amalgamated. This was the beginning of his disillusionment with the party—a development which eventually led to his breaking with it completely.

Although he had become increasingly cheesed off with the Communist Party, it was not until the year before he died that Jim officially resigned. I remember one summer day when the warm west wind was herding the cotton clouds into billowy bunches and the mosquitoes were rising like mist from the dew-damp grass, young Wilson MacAulay came scooting around the side of the house on his bicycle. There must have been no brake on the infernal machine for he could not stop and went skittering into Daddy,

Tom, and me, who were sitting on the back step.

"Damn you, you little christer!" yelled brother Tom, rubbing his shins. "Daddy, let me give him a good belt across the ear."

"Hold your coal, b'y," said Daddy, rather philosophically removing the tire mark from his boot. "Let's find out what the messenger brings before we behead him."

"Mr. MacLachlan would like to see Mr. Ross up home," said the lad, examining his bicycle for dents.

"Which Mr. Ross, did he say, b'y?" Daddy asked. "For as you see there are three of us here."

"He didn't say, Mr. Ross."

"Well, I guess we'd better all be going to be on the safe side."

Daddy gave the boy a penny and, when he had fetched his old black hat from inside the kitchen, we set out along the road for Glace Bay. Tom lasted only as far as town, where he was called aside by some of his buddies.

Daddy was visibly disgusted. "Amusement!" he scoffed. "That's what he lives for, that boy. Nothing but ball games and fights."

"It wouldn't do for everybody to be fanatics about politics and the union, Daddy," I said. "We'd probably be better off without him today anyhow. Besides, remember how you used to bawl me out for chasing skirt?"

"Indeed I do," he said with a toss of his head and just the faintest suggestion of a smile. "And no doubt I would still if you weren't hitched to that tiger cat."

"Do you really think of Marg that way, Da?" I asked. It was rare for him to talk about my marriage or, indeed, about much of anything beyond public affairs.

"Well, she's a spirited thing, you will admit that, Donnie," he said, taking out his pipe and slicing it into his mouth.

He stopped to strike a match on his boot and light up. The little cotton clouds were fluffed and creamy over his head and the blue pipe smoke drifted up past his black hat to be caught by the breeze and whisked away.

"I could never see you two together," the pipe came out, was shaken free of spittle, then clamped back between the yellow teeth, "but then look at your mother and me. A case of opposites attracting in the beginning I guess. It certainly was not a case of sharing a political philosophy."

"What do you suppose Jim wants?" I asked, abruptly changing the subject, for the drift of the conversation was making me uneasy. I knew that Ma and Daddy fought like hammer and tongs about union, church, politics, and moral values, but I didn't want to know anything more. All my life I had assumed that once the argument had subsided into a frosty silence all was forgiven, and once behind the bedroom door nothing else mattered. I did not want to hear anything different.

He took the bait. "I don't rightly know, Donnie," he said seriously. "But he's been troubled lately-you must have noticed it-and between ourselves..." he dropped his voice and shuffled a little closer, "I believe he's very sick."

"He's got very thin," I said, "but that could be old age creeping on. He must be over sixty-five now."

"Well, we're all getting no younger, b'y, but I'll bet Jim is consumptive. It's no wonder, too, the way he has driven himself, probably going without grub and always hustling around in the freezing cold barely dressed."

Brooding about these things, we reached Steeles Hill and struck out across the little track past the black and white cows in the field until we came to the big white house.

As soon as I took a look inside the door I felt out of place. There were about fifteen fellows inside—all of them staunch communists. Now it was clear which Mr. Ross he had been summoning: Daddy.

I made a motion as if to leave, but he waved me into an old horse-hair chair right by the door. Red Dan was leaning against the bookcase, another fellow was rolling a cigarette in the corner, two brothers were on the chesterfield, and Daddy and the others were dotted around the walls.

MacLachlan sat in a big armchair by the window where the brilliant sunshine was flashed and dappled over him by the dancing leaves of the tree whose branches occasionally scratched the glass. He looked terrible, all the more so because he was the only figure there who caught the sunlight, the rest of us almost merging into the gloom. He had almost no hair on the top of his head-just a few grey wisps-and it was very short and grizzled around his large ears. His face and nose seemed longer than usual, his cheeks were hollow, and his sunken, huge, limpid and brooding eyes stared beneath upper lids which dragged across them at an angle.

As he started to speak, the great moustache moved to reveal that, at least in his lower jaw, he had no teeth.

"Men," he said, his lowland burr as strong as ever, "I don't know about you, but I've had a bellyful of Joe Stalin, Tim Buck, and the whole shooting match."

There was silence as he peered around the room from under his great eyebrows, then he continued.

"I've been blind all these years. We've all been fools. Now I can think on it with a clear mind I see that all they ever did was aid our enemies. They backed Lewis and the International, they tried to sabotage the Miner, and I believe they just used our troubles and our tempests like parasites for their own advantage."

Most of the men merely looked at their boots, too embarrassed to say anything, but I noticed Daddy was staring straight at Jim, a look of pain on his face. Finally, one old fellow cleared his throat and spoke up.

"To tell you the truth, Jim, I've not been too comfortable with the party these last few years. The way they've treated yourself has been disgraceful."

"Oh, they were glad to get me to run as a candidate in last year's election, but you know they've never had much use for me." He rubbed his moustache with the back of his hand. "The line has changed so often I couldn't keep up with it. So I didn't try!"

There was a ripple of laughter at this last remark. The ice broken, several men started to talk at once.

"You did tend to take a little bit of an independent line, Jim. They don't like that."

More laughter.

"And the way they had Sandy MacKay spying on you!"

Mutters all round.

"Sending dossiers back, reporting on all your movements."

Curses.

"Well, I am free of them, boys," he said with a wave. "Cast them off like the old clothes they are."

He reached into his pocket and withdrew a folded piece of paper which he offered to the man nearest to him. "Here, this is a copy of a letter I sent to Comrade Buck a few weeks ago. In the absence of a speedy reply begging me to remain in the ranks I think I can safely say the party feels as relieved about it as I do!"

The laughter erupted again, but my father's voice came stabbing through the babble. His face was taut and strained, his eyes blinking furiously.

"Jim MacLachlan, I never thought I'd live to see this day. What are you proposing? That we drift rudderless from year to year, strike to strike? God knows we've had little enough faith, little enough to keep us together and now you want to take it away for personal reasons. Just because they didn't bow down to you and idolize you."

"Now, Tom, that's not fair!" Dan barked at him.

"Let the man speak," said Jim severely.

"I know the party's shortcomings as well as any man," Daddy continued, "but it's all we've got. Or does Jim want us to join the Tory Party? Jim, for Christ's sake, I've followed you these twenty-five years or more and stuck with you when there was many a man's hand against you. How can you do this?"

MacLachlan dragged his chair across the rug until he was close to Daddy and he put his hand on Daddy's knee.

"Tom," he said very quietly, "I'll overlook those things you said about this being personal. I think you know differently."

"I spoke in haste," Daddy muttered.

"I thought so." MacLachlan nodded. "But, Tom, you know we always said it was ideas that counted, not structures. We always agreed that organizations were only there to serve the cause. That's why we used the P.W.A. when we had nothing else and why we got rid of it when it became corrupt. That's why we turned our backs on Lewis with the Amalgamated. There was nothing sacred in the P.W.A., there was nothing sacrosanct about the U.M.W., and, believe me, there's nothing in holy writ that says the Communist Party is the only political vehicle available."

"What do you suggest?" My father was calm now.

"If you had some alternative, I would listen."

"That's just it," said Jim, sitting back in the chair, rubbing his palm over a bony knuckle, "I don't know what you want to do, boys, but I think it's time to start all over again. What we need is a new party. What we need is a political vehicle which will meet our needs here, an outfit we can run, whose policies we can set, with nobody breathing down our necks and telling us we can't do something because Moscow said so. There are things happening in the Prairies and in British Columbia, men are on the move, Woodsworth has been hammering away in Ottawa these fifteen years. There's hope, boys, I tell you there's hope yet!"

"What will you call the new party, Jim?"

"We'll hold a big convention, contact all the locals and we'll let them decide."

"How about the Cape Breton Labour Party?" I said, my first contribution to the debate.

"A good notion, Donnie," said Jim, his eyes lighting up. "We'll submit it to the convention and see what they think."

"Jim," I said, "I was never with you before, in the CP, but I'm with you now."

"Good lad," said Jim. "And, who knows, maybe you'll be able to say that you gave the new party its name."

I am able to say it because that is what they called it, but I must admit it was a relatively short-lived affair: the C.C.F. was on its way and soon took over where the others had left off.

So Jim was out of the Communist Party and Daddy with him. Jim's last brush with his former comrades came a few months later and it was something never to be forgotten.

The remaining communists in the area were staging a giant public meeting at the Firemen's Parlours in Glace Bay and the featured speaker was a communist Member of Parliament from West Fife in the industrial Scottish lowlands. Willie Gallagher was his name and I believe he was the only communist at Westminster at the time, having been elected in a by-election a year or two earlier.

In any event, we all went down to hear him, along with a good many others who did not follow the sponsoring party for, apart from Labour Party people like Daddy and me, I noticed a couple of known Liberals and at least one Tory in the audience. The hall was jam-packed and we were ushered to a couple of seats at the side where we wriggled into the heaving and, by now, heavily sweating mass of humanity. The only thing worse than the body odour was the smoke, which was hanging about our heads in great clouds with Daddy, of course, contributing his share from the old black briar.

Finally the chairman called for order and Mr. Gallagher was introduced. He was a fine speaker, first describing his triumphant election to Westminster and the amazing rate at which the party was growing in Britain, then turning to the usual fulsome praise about that workers' paradise known as the Soviet Union.

Then he moved closer to home, first boosting the local leadership of the CP, then launching into a lengthy and scathing attack on MacLachlan.

As the denunciation grew stronger and more vicious, so a muttering arose from the audience, Daddy and myself included in it.

Finally, Gallagher delivered his last few bitter insults, asking with a sneer, "And where is J.B. MacLachlan today, may I ask?"

Somewhere in the back of the hall a chair scraped as a bent old man stood up, his hand raised in mock salute.

"Here I am, Mr. Gallagher," came Jim's voice, clear and ringing.

You could have heard a feather fall as Jim stepped out into the aisle and walked forward. The look on Gallagher's face was worth a hundred dollars, but not worth near as much as it was when Jim was done with him.

He wiped the floor with him. In the last speech of his life MacLachlan, arms aloft, eyes blazing, held the audience spellbound as he tore the Communist Party to pieces in a systematic act of savage verbal butchery. When he had hammered the last nails into the coffin of Gallagher's arguments, he turned on heel and stalked out of the hall, the cheers of the crowd in his ears.

Within a little more than a year he was dead and four thousand people marched to pay tribute to this great man.

I was over in Greenwood Cemetery a few weeks

ago to tend the grave of one of our Protestant relatives and I had a look at Jim's headstone. It says:

OPEN THY MOUTH,
JUDGE RIGHTEOUSLY,
AND PLEAD THE CAUSE OF THE POOR
AND THE NEEDY

Whatever else anyone can say about Jim MacLachlan, he certainly did that.

I can well recall sitting in the tiny, gloomy back kitchen, peeling potatoes, when we heard the murmur coming up the row. Daddy sent my younger brother Alex to find out what was going on.

He was back in two shakes, his eyes wide, and his little face red with excitement. The whisper was travelling the whole island like a forest fire; painters called it out from the tops of ladders, tram drivers raucously yelled at passersby, engineers on the coal trains blew their whistles, and fat, old women passed it from fence to fence.

"Well, b'y," Daddy asked, looking up at Alex through his thick, bushy, white eyebrows, "is it money you're after wanting for your information or will you share for nothing?" Alex said hoarsely.

"Jim MacLachlan is dead,"

Father stared at him vacantly and we thought it had not registered until we saw a slight dewy fog veiling his red-rimmed eyes.

"There'll be strikes in heaven now," my mother said tartly from where she was standing at the stove.

"Quiet, woman," Daddy snapped, coming to life. "You don't know what you're saying."

He turned to Alex. "When and where, b'y?"

"At home, Da."

"Donnie, get my hat and put your boots on," he said to me very seriously. "We're away to pay our respects to one of the saints."

"Tom," my mother said sharply, "that's heresy!"

"No, woman, heresy is when people as ignorant as yourself worship names you've never heard of and people you know nothing about. I knew this man, Aggie, and I tell you he was a saint in our midst. If I lie, then God will deal with me in his own good time."

We ducked through the flimsy back porch and out into the unusually bright day, striding silently into the street and merging with the men who were gathered there. The men of the Dump seemed to be waiting for Daddy to lead them, and looking up the rows to the lines of company houses beyond I could see scores of men and boys leaving their homes and wandering aimlessly around the streets.

Daddy stood for a moment, his head inclined upwards, his eyes squinting against the sunlight, then he adjusted his hat, nodded curtly to the men and started the march. At the top of our street he paused and flicked a stone with his old stick.

"Donnie, it's time for me to die now," he said suddenly, his face looking harder and, in a way, younger than I had seen it in a long time.

"For Jeesake, Da," I said, feigning mirth, "you'll bury all of us yet, so don't be talking."

He said nothing, but turned forward again and fell into step.

We marched along the river, over the tracks, up the highway and down the long hill into Glace Bay. Everywhere men left their houses to join us as we wound through the dirty streets on our way to Steele's Hill.

You can't stop miners from talking if they've got something on their minds—and especially if they have a few in them—but today the men talked in a low, mumbling way like some giant bumble bee buried in the dusty petals of a flower.

The houses, usually dark green, chocolate brown, or black, went by, one after the other, almost all with long-faced, hushed women draped over the unpainted, fragile picket fences. Dogs and small children, who did not know what was happening and could not be expected to show any reverence for the occasion, strangely, weirdly, broke the atmosphere with yelps, cries, and loud questions.

I should have been thinking about Jim, for I knew and revered him almost as much as Daddy did, but I wasn't; I was thinking about my father and how serious he had been about predicting his own death. I tried to imagine my mother without him, our house without his huge, black boots just inside the door, the rocking chair without his stick propped against it, the worn kitchen table without his big chipped china cup. I had an awful, terrifying feeling that this man, who had exercised control over his and our lives, could somehow direct his own funeral proceedings.

I walked at his side, convinced that he would not be alive by winter. But it was two years before he finally went.

Daddy and Jim were alike in a number of ways. Both were self-educated, both dedicated and single-minded to the point of fanaticism, both with a stentorian voice—Jim's lowland Scots, Daddy's Newfoundland. They even looked a bit alike: tall, rangy, moustached, and nearly always in dark clothes, constantly gesturing with their bony hands.

Da died for want of breath, the doctor said, and I thought at the time that was put very simply and very well. Many's the time we had been out walking, going downtown dressed in our best Sunday black, or fooling around with the dog out on the cliffs, when he had stopped, doubled over with coughing, and on the ground at his feet would be a big pool of disgusting black slime. I still get that myself and I have been out of the pit quite a while.

Anyway, I guess Daddy had started to cough and could not get the coal dust up, so it choked him. I was on back shift and my mother would not tell me about it.

I do remember that no men filled the streets when Daddy died, but Black Jim and the Peglegs from next door came over and sat moodily in the kitchen muttering their sentiments over hot tea and cake which my mother, despite her obvious grief, had scurried around to prepare. They mentioned his death in the local, observed two minutes' silence "for our departed brother," then moved on to financial business and conditions in the main deep.

To this day, I do not know who missed him apart from the members of his small family, but it was very noticeable that the press statements from the union seemed to lack the literary tone they had once possessed. They say a man does not mind dying if he has a few dollars put away and a roof over his head and, of course, if he's a ripe old age. Hundreds did not have even that when they died.

I miss Daddy more as time passes and hold his memory dear and warm and close like a candle in the night. If there is another life for us I will not mind going if my father is there, although it would not surprise me if I found him organizing the angels into a union.

Daddy's memory is a treasure to me all the more because I know he died holding nothing against me and believing I carried on his name, committed, as he was, to a better life on earth.

My memory of my mother is bitter and anguished, cold and ash-grey, tortured and uncomfortable because she died resentful, not understanding and not forgiving. Pious but ignorant, she had been torn from the simplicity of country life and, scarcely before the apple sheen of womanhood had settled on her, was brought into a world she could not comprehend and of which she wanted no part. The unquestioned authority of parents, church, and nature, and the daily routine of the changing seasons, were brutally assaulted in a coal mining town whose life's breath was struggle and tumult.

Her days were made the more bitter by the fact that, even when she realized she had made a mistake in marrying him, Daddy would not allow her to aspire to the few good things which she thought urban life could offer. She could have tolerated the coal towns if she had been able to even dream of an official's job, a big house, nice clothes, and respectability, but my father's total being told her with every word, with every breath, with every movement, with every bead of sweat from his pores that even to dream was impossible.

Of course, I think Daddy was in the right, but it is a terrible thing to rob the dreams of others.

If anything, she resented me more than she did Daddy, because when I came along it gave her a momentary wave of fresh hope; that what was impossible for Daddy might be possible for me. Hope that I could be different, that I could go to college, become a lawyer or a doctor...or even a priest. Yes, she had even dared, in a fleeting ray of hopeshine, to think that her son might take the cloth and make amends for the rebelliousness, the savagery, the blasphemy, the turning on end of the natural laws of God.

But, to the unspeakable wormwood of the miscarriage of her desire, I was my father's son.

I was in Hamilton when I got the call to say that Ma was dying. I had taken off on my third childhood after one of my tiffs with Marg and was bumming around with some cronies who had moved there a few months previously. I was entirely in the wrong of the argument, as I usually was, and it is to Marg's great credit that she took me back at all. I was cranky, frustrated, empty of purpose, and, to make matters worse, it was the Jeanette time of the year.

As I put in the meaningless days at the coalface, scarcely aware of what I was doing or what was going on around me, I thought of the warm, lovelong days, the glitter of the lake in her eyes, the swish of the grass at her skirt. I remembered the call of the chickadee on her lips, and my hazy, cloudless and cornflower blue, skyborn life in her blood.

I silently raged against my middle age and against the days which could never be again. I got drunk, picked a fight with my long suffering by comparison wife and hotfooted it, irresponsibly and inevitably out of town.

"Ma is dying, come home." The message was simple. It was my brother Tom and he was drunk. Before I could ask for details he had rung off and the line was dead.

The sun was still strong in the small town, but I could feel the keen wintery smell in the smoke and the paint on the fences which ran out past the rickety houses and over the edge of the cliffs. The sounds of the traffic, the bells, the dogs, the freight yard carried on the breeze in a wintery way. I could taste the bite of the months to come.

Almost everybody I met stopped to give me a soft word about Ma. She had never had many friends, but though everyone knew her sharp, black, straight-laced ways, and most had kept clear of the edge of her wounding tongue, they respected her as they had respected Daddy, and maybe because of that.

Times were busy then, several dozen pits were grinding and chucking in our district, ten thousand men were working, few idle times, lots to eat and drink. It did not last very long but for a few brief, fat years the Dump and surrounding communities had hustled like children on the verge of perpetual Christmas.

The streets were crowded and the rail cars clanking and the taverns teeming when I left the train and strolled over the hill and into the Dump to see my dying mother. Not a drink had passed my lips, and I dreaded what last promises she might press upon me. I dreaded, too, Marg's accusing tone and withering eye.

They would not let me see her because she was sleeping, so I wandered out around the rows, along the cliffs, down to the shore and back through town, the gulls wheeling around my head, the dogs capering at my feet, and the voices of the people of the best place in the world brushing against my ears.

"Hello, Donnie!" Fiddler, and a wave across the street, turning into the U.M.W. offices.

"Look what the cat brought in." Bill MacGregor from the barbershop. Then quickly: "Sorry about your Ma."

"Back again, eh, b'y? Too bad about your Ma." Old Mrs. Wingate, bent and bowed, and burrowing through the crowd.

"By the jumpin' Joe Jesus, Donnie Ross!" John Dan and a punch on the arm. "They said you'd be back. I'll be up to the house before long, tell her."

"Donnie, that you, b'y? Do you be's coming with me to help me home?" Allie Shivers, reeling, and second-hand rum in my face.

"Good day, Donald." Note of surprise, Leo Talbot, well-dressed and walking with importance. "A fine woman, your mother."

"Donnie!" Scream from across the way. Hughie MacNeil with a gang. "Come join us for a beer, b'y!"

Whisper from Clarence Binder in Hughie's ear. Telling him about my Ma. Hughie, silent, turning away.

"Is it really you?" Bumping around the corner into old Adam. Dear, ancient Adam, warm and nearly blind, clasping me to him like a son. "Soon be my turn, Donnie, soon be my turn."

When I got back she was dead. Marg told me that the last occasion on which she had mentioned me the words had been of recrimination.

I could not blame her. She died empty of vision, robbed of hope, her soul a sour, aching void. I had stolen her dreams and she would not forgive the thief.

15: A blessed arrangement

It is getting cold and very soon it will be dark. If I stay here any longer the pin-point lights will go on one by one in these rickety old houses and the lamp at the top of the row will throw that mushy golden pool around the dog that's sniffing at its base. Dozens of kitchens twinkling into the evening.

Our light shines differently from the others, kind of greenish because of the plastic curtains in the kitchen windows. It is a mark of distinction, a badge, an unwritten name-plate behind which the old oil cloth, the old rocking chair, the old, plain, square table may look like many others, but feel like none. A kitchen that is seventy years old and has a big, hot range in it is a sight more welcoming than an infra-red eye-level grill in avocado with chrome trim.

Our kitchen is like no other in the world; it smells right. After getting chilled to the bone up here on this cliff it will be good to set my foot over the creaking floor and stand my rear end to the stove.

I have decided what to do. I am going to propose a compromise—imagine, me compromising! I am going to suggest that Marg and I go to live with Ruby and Tom in Toronto and give the old house to Will and Annie. What we will do is spend six months of the year at clean-as-Sunday Agincourt Crescent and six months here with Will. What could be fairer? Indeed, the solution strikes me with such blinding clarity I am amazed it did not occur to me before.

When she sees that I have come half way Marg will go along and Will is not likely to raise any objection if we spend the first stretch with Ruby. Ruby and her Tom will bless the arrangement, especially after they have put up with my eccentricities for half a year at a time, and even the children will be better off for not being lumbered with an old bear all year long. I think it will work.

Way out, there is a big ship gliding along the edge of the blackness, its tiny lights pricking the cold sky. The wind is rising and the salt smell is getting stronger, and I can hear that quiet rattling sound made by the water on the small pebbles. When the breeze is right the faint noises of the pit come drifting across the bay and the lights are going on all over town.

Someone is playing Jim Reeves on a record player in the Fourth Row, the MacMullens' old yellow dog is beginning to howl, and everything I love is pressing in on me from all sides like spirits whispering on the wind. Grown men do cry.

I am going away to live with my daughter, whom I dearly love, with my wife who loves me. I am going to leave this cliff, the windswept rows with their chimney smoke captured in nervous wisps, the ugly, lovely town on the edge of the world.

I am going to say goodbye to Spiv, Hookey, Skinthedoors, Duce, Bull, Bo-bo, the Fatterhooks, the Pats, the Clams, the Goats, the Papooses, the Spiders, Cock-eye, Stub, the Minute Hand, Burnt Rory, Corny, Crooked Billy, the Birds, the Cats, the Stumps, Bogfoot, Biscuitfoot, Black Joe, Peglegs, Rory the Bear, Danny the Moose, Red Mick, the Busy Bees and Jack the Tiger, but I'll be back.

By Jesus, I'll be back!

Jeremy Akerman

Author's note

You will not find the Dump on any map of Cape Breton Island, nor will the Glory Hole or "A" and "B" collieries appear on plans of the Dominion Coal Company or its successor the Cape Breton Development Corporation. None of the Donald Rosses in the Cape Breton telephone directory is the narrator of this story.

The following names which appear in the text are real, historical figures:

J.B. MacLachlan, J.S. Woodsworth, Reverend W.T. Mercer, Norman Bethune, Marion Davies, Mohandus Gandhi, Randolph Hearst, Wally O'Hearn, W.L. Mackenzie King, Ernest LaPointe, Roy Wolvin, John W. MacLeod, Alex MacKay, Arthur Meighen, "Moscow" Jack MacDonald, Bobby Baxter, Tim Buck, Red Dan Livingstone, E.H. Armstrong, J.E. McClurg, Colonel Eric MacDonald, Captain D.A. Noble, Silby Barrett, H.C. LeVatte, Paddy Muise, John C. Douglas, Dan Willie Morrison, John L. Lewis, Joe Nearing, Bishop Morrison, Angus MacEachern, Carl Haley, Angus MacDonald, Dougie MacDonald, Tommy Ling, Gilbert Watson, Michael O'Handley, William Davis, V.I. Lenin, J. Stalin, Senator Joseph McCarthy, Sir Andrew

Duncan, Edgar Rhodes, Sandy MacKay, Willie Gallagher, John W. Moffat.

All other characters are fictitious, though many
readers might think they recognize them. This is in-
evitable in a place like the Cape Breton coalfields,
and especially where so many people carry the same
names.

If some of the anecdotes seem familiar to any of
the older miners, it is because I have adapted them
from the many yarns I heard in the cozy back kitchens of New Aberdeen, Passchendaele, the Hub,
Cranberry, and Fourteen Yard. For this I make no
apology: they were great yarns and should be
shared.

If anybody thinks they recognize themselves in
this story, and is offended, I can only say that this is
far from my intention. If it is anything, this book is a
work of love and a song of praise.

Special thanks to my friends Silver Donald
Cameron and Kenzie MacNeil for their advice and
encouragement at a time when I was ready to heave
the whole thing into the nearest fire.

Jeremy Akerman
Halifax, 1980

About the author

Jeremy Akerman is an adoptive Nova Scotian who has lived in the province for 58 years (as of 2022). In that time he has been an archaeologist, a radio announcer, a politician, a senior civil servant, a newspaper editor and a film actor.

He is painter of landscapes and portraits, a singer of Irish folk songs, a lover of wine, and a devotee of history, especially of the British Labour Party.